JAKE

by Alfred Slote

ArborvilleBooks

Ann Arbor · Michigan

To the Bimbo's team, who refused to be dissolved, who sought for and found a coach.

1.

My name is Jake Wrather, which doesn't mean much to you, and it doesn't mean much to me either. I never knew my father who gave me my last name, and my mother left two years ago to visit down south and never came back. I room with my Uncle Lenny and he doesn't care about anything except music. We get along fine because I don't care about anything except baseball. He plays his music in Detroit at night while I'm sleeping, and I play baseball during the daytime while he's sleeping, so it works out fine. I like being on my own. Nobody tells me when to go to bed, what to eat. I do what I want to do. I take what I want.

I got an Al Kaline glove and nobody gave me that, or my bat either. I found my bat in a kid's hands one day over at Sampson Park. I convinced him that I needed it more than he did. I found my glove in a department store when no one was looking.

Does this sound like bragging? If it does, I don't mean it to. I don't steal except when I have to. I'm eleven years old. I don't want to grow up a crook. Just a ball player, and a ball player needs his tools: a bat and a glove.

I don't have many friends. One good one: John Fulton, the catcher on our team. He's a tough, quiet kid and we get along fine. I eat at his house a lot. Mrs. Fulton's got used to my coming around their house about dinnertime. She always grins and says: "Jake, I think we can manage an extra place at the table. Would you like to stay for supper?"

And I always grin and say: "Don't mind if I do."

Sometimes I get tired of cooking myself hamburgers and hot dogs. And Mrs. Fulton is a darn good cook. She's a lot better cook than she is a baseball coach.

That's right. Mrs. Fulton, up until a little while ago, was the coach of our Little League team. And she didn't know a thing about baseball. I mean, she once asked Ned Franks who plays left field: "Ned, are you a fielder or a batter?"

Old Ned just gulped and said: "Both, Coach."

Mrs. Fulton didn't want to be coach. She just liked coming to the games and sitting in a canvas chair and reading the paper and when John would get up, she'd put the paper down and watch. Or sometimes she'd keep score. We taught her how to do that. But she came to all the games and she was the only parent that did.

And when we lost our coach and they threatened to disband the team unless we got an adult coach, there was only one move to make: ask Mrs. Fulton to coach.

League rules said you had to have an adult coach, but they didn't say that adult had to be a man.

Fact was: we couldn't get a man. Not a father on the club had time to coach us, and my Uncle Lenny who could coach us, since he was such a hot-shot college athlete in all sports, was way out of it in his music world. It was either break up the team or get Mrs. Fulton.

We got Mrs. Fulton. She thought it was a ridiculous thing, and it was, but all she had to do was shake hands with the opposite coach, discuss ground rules (like when the foul balls were out of play, or whether balls hit into the tall grass were doubles or homers) and then go sit and read the paper.

I ran the team. I'm not bragging. I'm just stating a fact. I ran the team. Not because I was the best player on the team—I wasn't. Danny Kohl, our shortstop, could outfield me, Andy Black our right fielder could outhit me. Jeff Bigler, our hot-tempered first baseman could outrun me, Dick Williams our center fielder had a better arm, and Jerry Jones our ace pitcher was better all around than me. But I could do one thing better than any of them: I could outfight them, outgrowl them, outhustle them. I could chew them out. When they were in danger of falling apart, I could keep them together. And I liked doing it. I was probably the youngest coach in baseball history, but it didn't bother me. We were off to a good start. Three victories and no games lost, Mrs. Fulton was reading her paper during the games, and everyone was happy except the opposing teams. None of them liked the Print-Alls— that's the name of our team; we're sponsored by a printing company —because we were a loose-as-a-goose outfit that would as soon knock you down as spit at you. But they couldn't do anything about it. I guess the combination of nine tough hard-nosed ball players being "led" by a lady coach, with a big floppy hat and a newspaper under her arm, was just too much to take.

Finally, one coach didn't take it. His name was McLeod and his team was the McLeod Builders. They were in second place right behind us, and I guess it all got to be too much for Mr. McLeod and his team.

2.

LAST YEAR IN THE ARBORVILLE TEN-YEAR-OLD LEAGUE WE beat the McLeod Builders without much trouble. They've only got three or four real ball players. But this year, their ace pitcher Pat McLeod—the coach's son—got himself a little curve ball. We'd heard about it before we saw it. Jerry, our ace, didn't have a curve yet, though Tony Parker our second pitcher had one that wasn't much good. Still, Arborville isn't a big city, and word soon got around that Pat McLeod had a curve ball that could come right at you, and then when you bailed out to avoid getting hit, the ball would drop over the plate. When we met the Builders Tuesday night at West Park, they were two wins and no losses, having played one less game than us, and in second place.

We were up for the game, talking it up. Mrs. Fulton was reading her newspaper and there were about twenty adults in the stands behind home plate, all parents of the Builders. Mr. McLeod was a tall red-faced guy who wore a baseball cap and was always shouting down at his players. They were a well-trained team, you could see that right away, and much improved over last year. He ran that team like a machine, but we had the better ball players, and if Jerry was on with his rising fast ball, it would be as easy as picking peaches.

The trouble with that first game against the Builders was that Jerry wasn't on. His first pitch of the game was in the dirt.

John Fulton blocked it, even though he didn't have to, but our hearts sank. When Jerry started out this way he usually got worse before he got better. It then depended on how many runs we could score before he got some sort of pitching rhythm again.

Playing third base, I liked it less than anyone. When Jerry was wild it meant I covered home on wild pitches because when Jerry got wild he also got moody and wouldn't budge off the pitcher's mound.

Jerry walked the McLeod lead-off batter Tim Johnson to start the game. The next kid up was Larry Esch who was a lefty and drag-bunted all the time. Larry hadn't got an honest hit since he started playing in the Arborville Recreation League three years ago. You won't believe this, but I heard his father call out from the stands once, offering Larry a dollar if he got a swinging hit. Larry got all tight and clutched and struck out.

Walking Tim Johnson was one thing, but walking a powder-puff hitter like Esch would be terrible.

I called "time" and went over to talk with Jerry, to calm him down, for he was kicking the dirt already, disgusted with himself. I felt like kicking him. Jeff Bigler trotted over from first, and that would be no help because Bigler was twice as excitable as Jerry. John Fulton came out from his catcher's position looking so worried I almost laughed.

John could see a whole afternoon of digging Jerry's fast balls out of the dirt. Catching Jerry had made John the best fielding catcher in the eleven-year-old league.

No sooner did we get together than Mr. McLeod shouted: "Make them move the game along, Ump."

"What's eating him?" Bigler said.

"Ignore him," I growled. I turned to Jerry. "These guys are bums. What're you throwing the shovel ball at them for?"

Jerry gave me his hard look, which didn't bother me one bit. Jerry's big and strong but we both knew I could wrestle him into the ground. Jerry and Andy are the other two black players besides me and they're both very different from each other. Jerry's moody and gifted. I mean, he can hit, run, field, pitch. And he's going to be a great basketball player. Andy's big and strong and like a rock. He never gets mad, never gets happy. I figure him for a fullback. Being black players on the team, you'd think we'd be buddy-buddy. But we're not. No one's buddy-buddy with Jerry because of his temper.

"Listen, man," I said to Jerry, "old Fulton here's got good at handling that old shovel ball of yours but in the end you'll bust his hands."

John's worried expression changed into a smile. It had taken little John three whole games to figure out that a shovel ball was a ball that dug holes in front of the plate before it hopped up and hit you in the neck.

Jerry didn't think I was funny. "You take care of your position, Jake, and I'll take care of mine."

"I got no position to take care of if you keep throwing shovel balls."

"Hey, Ump," Mr. McLeod bellowed from his third-base coaching box, "make them play ball. It'll get dark in an hour."

The relatives in the stands started shouting, too, that we were stalling. Truth was, it did get dark early at West Park, and there were no lights here. But I wasn't going to leave Jerry to kick dirt and rattle himself.

Every adult was shouting at the umps to move us along, except our coach Mrs. Fulton. She was reading the paper, oblivious to it all.

Jerry kicked the dirt disgustedly. "I'll get 'em over, Jake."

"Don't throw so hard," Bigler advised.

Jerry glared at Jeff Bigler. "Don't you start telling me what to do. Jake's bad enough."

"C'mon, kids," the plate umpire called out, "let's play ball."

"Oh, shut up," Bigler said through gritted teeth.

I had to grin. We were eleven years old. The plate ump was about fifteen and he was calling us kids.

"C'mon, Ump," Mr. McLeod shouted, "time's wasting."

"Quit stalling, Print-Alls."

"You guys come to play ball or talk?"

"Looks like a ladies' sewing circle."

Mr. McLeod turned and spoke loudly for the benefit of the McLeod team's parents in the stands: "This is what happens when a team plays without a coach."

If he was also talking for Mrs. Fulton's benefit, she

missed it completely. She just turned the pages of her newspaper.

"Boy, I'd like to sic your Uncle Lenny on that guy," Bigler said.

"Forget him," I said. "He's all wind. You get them over, Jerry, or I'll stomp you after the game."

Jerry grinned. "You're always stomping someone, Jake."

"I mean it," I said. And walked back to my position. "This kid can't hit. He's a bunter," I shouted.

And to prove my point, I moved in along the third baseline until I was only about twenty feet from the batter.

"Look at the hot dog, guys," the McLeod team began shouting.

"Hot dog."

"Show-off."

"Hit it down his throat, Larry."

"Cream him, Larry."

Jerry was grinning as he put his foot on the slab.

"Don't change-up on me, Jones," I shouted. For if he did that, Esch would really ram it down my throat. I was counting on Jerry's fast ball.

He threw it hard and it went into the dirt. John Fulton blocked it with his body, keeping the ball in front of him, pounced on it, and cocked his arm for a throw to second, but Tim Johnson wasn't going.

Mr. McLeod yelled at him for not going.

"The next time that ball's in the dirt, you go," he shouted. A mean-type father-coach, I thought.

"Pitcher's wild," their bench started chanting.

"Pitcher's going up, up, up. ... ."

"Hey, pitcher, pitcher, pitcher. ... ."

"C'mon, Jerry," I called out, "no batter in there."

"Lay it in the old glove, Jerry," I heard John call out from behind the plate.

Jerry looked fussed. He kicked some more dirt as though that would improve hit pitching.

I looked over at Mrs. Fulton. She was still reading the paper. Maybe a little humor would loosen Jerry up.

"Hey, Mrs. Fulton," I called out, "you think we ought to put this dude on?"

Mrs. Fulton looked up startled. "Put him on what?" she said.

That cracked Jerry up. He threw the next pitch five feet over the batter's head and Tim Johnson took second standing up.

Jeff Bigler screamed at me. "Stop clowning, Jake."

At shortstop Danny Kohl shuffled his feet nervously. "C'mon, Jerry. These guys are nothings."

"Pitcher's wild, wild, wild," the McLeod kids started chanting again.

"Take another pitch, Larry," Mr. McLeod called out, with a big grin. "He won't get it in there."

"Hey, the hot dog's moving back," one of their kids called out.

I was moving back because with a man on second and Jerry throwing those terrible pitches, we might have a play at third. But I didn't go all the way back because Esch would surely bunt if he could.

Jerry didn't give him a chance to bunt. He threw the next pitch in the dirt, too.

"He's coming, Jake," Danny shouted.

I hustled back. John had the ball blocked. He was quick as a cat. He grabbed it and fired the ball down to me. A perfect throw. On my left side, my glove side, and I was waiting for Tim Johnson. He came in headfirst which was too bad for him because I slammed the ball socko onto his head and Tim never even reached the bag.

"You're out," the bases ump shouted, jerking his thumb in the air.

Johnson just lay there. Mr. McLeod ran over. He pushed me out of the way even though I wasn't in the way.

"Hey, mister, watch it," I said.

"Tim, are you OK?"

Tim Johnson nodded. He was OK, just humiliated like he should be, trying to steal third on John Fulton and Jake Wrather. And the only reason he'd gone was because his coach had screamed at him for not going before when a ball was in the dirt. If anyone was to blame for me putting the skull tag on, it was the coach.

Mr. McLeod straightened up and came over to me. His hands were balled into fists. Was he going to hit me? I couldn't believe it. I stepped back. I wasn't ready to take on a six-foot adult, not yet. For the first time in my life I wished my Uncle Lenny was around. Nobody, but nobody tangled with Lenny.

The bases ump, a tall skinny fifteen-year-old kid, stepped between us.

"Take it easy, Mr. McLeod," he said.

"If I ever catch that Wrather kid tagging one of my players like that again—"

"He came in headfirst," I said. "Where else could I tag him?"

"You didn't tag him. You hit him."

I didn't say anything because there was a bit of truth to that. But that's baseball. You play hard-nosed and you beat guys. You manhandle the team you can manhandle. You get them scared of you, and you pull your own team together. Look at Jerry right now. All the itchiness was gone out of him. That skull tag straightened him out just the way it did the runner—only for a good purpose.

"Anyway," I said, and winked at Jerry, "everyone knows the skull's the hardest part of a guy's head."

That got a big laugh from our guys, but Mr. McLeod got all red again.

"How about throwing him out of the game?" he asked the bases ump.

I got scared then. We only had nine guys. And you could get tossed out for sassing a coach.

But the ump shook his head. He turned to me. "That's a bad joke, Jake. OK, guys, now let's play ball."

Mr. McLeod wasn't happy. He wanted me out of the game. He stomped back to his coaching box, complaining loudly for the benefit of the fans.

"Sore loser," Jeff Bigler called out from first. McLeod whirled, but I whirled faster. I still had the ball and I threw the ball at Bigler.

"Shut up, Bigler," I shouted.

Bigler couldn't talk and catch at the same time and he caught the ball and had the sense to shut up. He tossed it to Danny who tossed it to Tony who threw it to me and I threw it to John Fulton and there we were tossing the ball around the infield as though nothing had happened. Mr. McLeod stood there, furious but baffled, and finally he walked off the field, muttering again how teams without coaches shouldn't be permitted in the league.

I was pretty sure it was Mr. McLeod who had tried to get our team broken up when Mr. Parker changed jobs and couldn't coach us anymore. McLeod called a meeting with Mr. Fredericks, the league president, but by then we'd come up with Mrs. Fulton and they didn't know what to say.

All in all, fighting to keep ourselves together as a team had really made us a tightly-knit ball club. Most teams carry fifteen or sixteen players because when summer vacation starts, kids go to camp. None of our guys go to camp. That's good. But what's bad is that sometimes a guy gets sick or, worse, gets thrown out of a game. Bigler especially was very good at getting thrown out of games last year. League rules say you can play with eight guys but not with seven. So I guard the team real carefully after Bigler gets thrown out. Especially Jerry, because Jerry's temper is almost as explosive as Jeff's. I'm the team cop. My job is to keep everyone cool and loose.

Like right now, we're cool and loose and the skull tag did it. Jerry's got three balls and no strikes on Esch but he looks more relaxed. He knows he's got a hot fielding team behind him, and knowing that he can get a rhythm and chuck away. It's when a pitcher starts thinking he's got to do it all himself that he tightens up and loses his stuff.

With no runner on base, I moved down the line again until I was only fifteen feet away from Esch. I was playing the position like a softball third baseman in a fast pitch game.

"Ram it down his throat, Larry," they yelled.

"Let's see that little old bunt, Larry," I said, grinning.

Jerry kicked, reared, and fired. It smoked in for a strike. Esch never took the bat off his shoulders.

Our hearts lifted; our voices sang out.

"Way to go, big Jerry."

"Throw the hummer, big Jerry."

Jerry poured a second strike in there that Larry just blinked at. The McLeod voices died down. They wouldn't touch Jerry now.

"Keep burning it in there, big man," I said, and spat toward the McLeod bench. They were very silent.

Jerry kicked, reared, and instead of throwing the smoke ball, he threw a change-up. Larry Esch who couldn't see the fast ball, got a good look at this. And there he was, swinging toward left field with me fifteen feet away.

Keerack! I ducked, sticking my glove up to protect my face. The ball breathed hot air over me. I turned to see where it had gone.

"It's in your glove, Jake," Jerry said, laughing.

"Way to go, Jake," John Fulton said. "Let's go over

those signals again, Jerry."

"Nope," Jerry said, grinning, and I knew he'd thrown that change-up on purpose. To keep me on my toes.

"I got a notion to belt you one," I said, throwing the ball back to him.

Jerry laughed. "Had to see how quick you really were, man. You're quick, OK."

"Next one Jake's going to catch with his head between his legs," Tony Parker called out.

"Haha," I said.

Even silent old Andy in right field got into the act: "My, oh my, Jake," he called out.

I growled at all of them, but deep down I was pleased. We were loose now. The skull tag and the crazy catch had done it. Pat McLeod, their pitcher and a good hitter, was up next. But Jerry reared back and poured the smoker three times right across the plate, and after the third pitch John Fulton flipped the ball up to McLeod and said: "Fast, ain't he, Pat?"

And whooping it up, we ran in.

"What's the batting order, Coach?" I asked Mrs. Fulton. She put down the newspaper and reached for the lineup I'd made out.

"Kohl, Parker, Wrather, Black."

"Way to call them, Coach," I said to her.

Mr. McLeod who was crossing the diamond thought I was sassing him again. He turned and gave me a dirty look.

Bigler laughed. We all laughed. Mr. McLeod got red

in the face. It was a dumb thing. We were making a real enemy out of him, and in just a few minutes we were going to pay a price for it.

3.

Pat McLeod's curve ball was all it was cracked up to be. It came right at you and dipped away. Danny Kohl our lead-off hitter was the first to get fooled. He pulled away from a pitch that hit his bat and rolled down the third baseline. Danny was out by twenty feet.

"Lucky," I growled at the third baseman.

Jerry grinned. "You're sure one tough dude today, Jake."

"I'm tough every day," I said. "C'mon, Tony, do your thing."

That was my way of telling Tony that McLeod would be an easy guy to bunt on. It's hard to bunt the high fast-ballers like Jerry, but all you got to do is follow that curve around with your bat and drop the ball in the grass. Tony's fast, too. After Bigler, he's the fastest man on the team.

"Watch the bunt, Joe," the McLeod left fielder called out to the third baseman.

"I'm taking the bunt sign off," Ned Franks, coaching at third, said. He went into a series of signals that didn't mean a thing, but got us laughing.

"Make 'em quit clowning, Ump," Mr. McLeod called out.

"Batter up," the ump said.

Tony Parker stepped in. Pat McLeod went to a small

wind-up and in came the lazy slow curve. Tony squared around to bunt. The third baseman came charging in. With great reflexes, Tony pulled his bat back and slapped it by him, down the third baseline. Fair ball. Tony made the turn around first and then tore for second. The throw was high. He slid in for a smart-looking double.

"Way to go, Tony."

"That's the way to suck them in and blow it by them."

"Hey, Pitcher, your pants are falling down."

"Hey, McLeod, your socks smell."

Mr. McLeod was standing up, looking angrily at us. "They're not allowed to call anyone's name, Ump," he said.

It was an Arborville Recreation League Rule. The ump told us to shut up, and for a few seconds we did.

Then we started shouting again.

"Woah, Pitcher."

"Hit it out of here, Jake."

"That's a meatball curveball, Jake."

"My grandmother throws a better curve than that, Pitcher."

I swung my bat with the heavy red doughnut. I looked over their outfield. A nice hole between center and left. There was a small ravine back there. Last year I'd hit a ball out there and it rolled down the ravine and the center fielder was fifteen minutes looking for it. There was no special rule about that ravine. You got what you took. That's my rule of life, too.

"Batter up," the ump said. "C'mon, Batter, get in there."

"Don't rush me," I said. I tossed the doughnut away.

It rolled right up and into the equipment bag which was lying on the ground.

The guys applauded me. "Hole in one," Bigler said.

"Quit stalling," said Mr. McLeod. "If you had a coach, you'd be playing baseball instead of showboating."

He was getting madder and madder and his team was getting tighter and tighter. We were real loose.

I looked down at Ned Franks for a phony signal. He gave me one. He stuck his tongue out at me. Everyone cheered. I thought Mr. McLeod would bust a gut, he was so angry. That was fine. The angrier he got, the worse his team would play.

I stepped in, and as I dug in, Pat McLeod quick-pitched me.

"Strike one," the ump said.

"Wait a second."

"Quick pitch," Bigler shouted, jumping up. So did Jerry. Everyone was off the bench shouting.

"Don't take any lip from them, Ump," Mr. McLeod said.

The ump didn't. He didn't even look at me. I dug in, not taking my eyes off Pat McLeod. He looked a little embarrassed. Over at second, Tony took a big lead. They weren't doing much to keep him close. Pat glanced at him and then sent his pitch toward the plate. Out of the corner of my eye I saw Tony take off for third. He had it made so easily I wouldn't have to protect him with a swing. But if the ball was in there I'd give it a ride. It was a lazy old curve up around my eyes. I let it go.

"Strike two," the ump said.

"What?"

"Strike two."

"You're kidding."

"Strike two."

"Hey, man, you can't do that."

"Throw him out of the game, Ump."

"Don't sass the ump, Jake, he'll throw you out of the game."

"What's the matter, Jake? Can't you see a strike?"

It was the Builders shouting. Our team, the Print-Alls, were silent. Like we couldn't believe what was happening. I couldn't believe it either. Bigler was going into motion though. Coming toward the ump.

"Ump," Jeff said, "I got another pair of glasses."

The ump turned toward him, his hand extended. Jeff Bigler was two seconds away from being thrown out of the game.

"Shut up, Bigler," I snarled.

Jeff stopped, the ump hesitated, and then Danny Kohl got Jeff and led him back to the bench.

I looked at the plate ump. He didn't look particularly mean-looking before, but he did now. A lot of thoughts went through my mind, but I didn't say them.

I had two phony strikes on me.

"Get in there, Batter," he said.

Warily I stepped in, never taking my eyes off Pat McLeod. Tony took a big lead off third. McLeod came down with his pitch. It was a curve that broke too soon.

Way outside. But I couldn't afford to take a chance, not with two strikes, so I leaned across the plate and tapped it foul.

I looked back at the ump and asked in my friendliest voice: "Would that have been a strike, Ump?"

He didn't answer me.

"That was right over the outside corner, Jake," the McLeod catcher said.

"Yeah," I grunted.

I dug in. McLeod had his foot on the rubber. Tony came down the line at third. Pat stepped off the rubber and Tony hopped back to the bag. Tony could steal home. If he got a good jump I knew he would, even though our big hitter Andy Black was up next. The ump was not fair, so it might be easier to steal yourself than be robbed by him. Stealing home was a matter of jump more than speed, and Tony was good at getting the jump. I could see Pat trying to work it out in his mind. Was Tony bluffing? Would he really try to steal home with only one out and the number three and four hitters up there? He wanted to go to a full wind-up. Get a little something extra on his curve.

He decided Tony was bluffing because he went to his full wind-up and here came Tony, and he kept coming. For a split second, Pat McLeod hesitated—it was a balk—everyone shouted balk. And then he threw. He was too late. Tony was crossing the plate standing up, the ball bounced on the plate and into the catcher's glove. By the time the catcher put the tag on Tony he was across the plate.

"You're out," the ump shouted.

"What?" I screamed.

"And you're out, too," he said to me. "That was strike three."

I was stunned. So was Tony. We both stood there like statues, our mouths open. Even the McLeod kids were surprised. They made no move to come in. Their pitcher had balked. Even a blind man could have seen that. The runner had stolen home, the ball had bounced on the plate —and somehow the ump was giving them two outs on it.

Everything broke loose at once. Our team went wild. Jeff Bigler began pushing the ump, Tony was crawling up his back. Jerry who was as big as he was, had his path of retreat to the backstop cut off, and was pushing him toward the diamond.

And I just stood there pounding my bat on the plate, shouting: "It hit the plate."

I wouldn't leave.

Everyone was screaming at once. Only Dick Williams, our left fielder, was cool enough to think of appealing to the bases ump.

He ran over to the bases ump and begged him about the balk, about the ball bouncing on the plate, about the late tag.

The bases ump looked embarrassed. He just shook his head. "The plate ump calls balks, fellas. They were all plays at the plate. I can't call them."

So we went back to the plate ump, shouting at him, a

wave of kids yelling.

Through it all, I heard Mr. McLeod call out: "Throw them out of the game, Ump. Don't let them push you around."

But maybe what was most unbelievable was that while a knot of kids with Print-Alls written on their backs surged around the umpire screaming and shouting, the McLeod Builders' team stayed in the field. They couldn't believe it either.

If anything in the world should have convinced the ump he'd made a rotten call it was that.

Mr. McLeod saw it, too. He called out: "What're you guys waiting for? You're up at bat."

"Shut up," Bigler shouted at him.

"Who're you telling to shut up?" Mr. McLeod asked.

"He's telling you to shut up," Jerry said angrily.

Mr. McLeod turned to the plate umpire. "I want to know how much abuse a coach has got to take before the umpire will throw a player out?"

The ump said: "I want to talk to their coach."

"They don't have a coach. That's the whole trouble."

"We do, too, have a coach," Jerry said, "and she knows a lot more than you do about baseball."

"That's it, fella," the ump said. "You're out of the game."

"What for?" Jerry said. "For saying our coach knows more than their coach?"

"You're out for arguing, shouting, pushing me. I should have thrown you out of the game five minutes ago."

Jeff sprang forward. "You're an ass, Ump. You—"

I jumped Jeff, and clamped my hand over his mouth. "He didn't mean it, Ump. He's having a fit." I pulled Jeff off to the side. "Listen, you jackass. He just threw Jerry out. That leaves us with eight men. If he throws you out we forfeit. Use your head, man."

Jeff was shaking mad. I held him tight. Danny Kohl began shooing everyone away from the plate. Andy Black helped me with Jeff.

"Time, Ump," I said to the bases ump who was just standing there shaking his head sadly.

"Time," he said.

"We got to have a team meeting. Over here, guys."

"Jake, what's going on?"

That was Mrs. Fulton. She'd finally put the paper down.

"We're getting killed by the umpire."

"Has he been unfair?"

"Unfair?" Bigler said. "He's a dirty rat."

"Shut up, Bigler," I said.

"I'm going to let the air out of his bike tires," Ned Franks said.

"Shut up, all of you," I yelled, and they finally shut up. "Listen, we're in a big hole now. We got to win this game and we got to win it without Jerry."

"How can we?" Bigler said.

"We can," I growled at him. "We can beat these guys, but if we get mad, we're sunk. That's just what he wants us to do. Look at Mr. McLeod, grinning all over. He got rid of our big pitcher. Now all he's got to do is get rid of one more guy and we forfeit the game. Are you gonna hand them this game, Jeff?"

"No," Bigler said, "but how're we gonna beat these guys with that ump calling plays like that?"

"OK, that's a good question. Mr. McLeod's got him under his thumb. So we got to scare him a little. Mrs. Fulton, can you come up to the plate with me while Tony warms up with John?"

"What do you want me to do?"

I told her what I wanted her to say to the ump and she nodded and we went up to the plate. The two umps were talking, with the bases ump doing most of the talking. The plate ump looked unhappy, like he was getting a royal chew-out.

"Excuse me," I said politely, "but our coach wants to say a few words to you."

Mrs. Fulton cleared her throat and then she told them what I'd told her to say. That she was going to write down every bad call that was made from now on, that we were going to play this game under protest, and that she and her husband intended to speak to Mr. Fredericks, the league president, about this game unless the umpiring became fairer.

She said it well. In fact she got angry as she talked, as though she really knew what was going on and was upset. In spite of everything, I had a hard time not grinning.

Neither of the umps said anything, though I thought the bases ump was grinning a little in his eyes. Then Mrs. Fulton went back to her chair, took out a piece of paper and a pencil, and looked very grim and businesslike, ready to write down every bad call.

I went back to third. Dick Williams came in to play second in place of Tony Parker who was now pitching. Jerry sat on the sidelines, quiet and alone watching us. For a crazy second I thought he was crying, but he was too tough to cry. He felt bad. They had suckered him and he knew it.

Boy, did we owe that McLeod team a few things. The next guy who came sliding into third wasn't going to get up at all. And the guy I slid into was going to be out for the season.

I checked out my team. Andy was playing center-right, Ned was deep in left. Tony didn't have Jerry's fast ball. They'd get around on him OK. They'd hit him. We'd have to be ready.

4.

ON SOME OTHER TEAMS TONY PARKER MIGHT HAVE BEEN the number one pitcher. He had good control, a curve ball, and he was smart. He remembered who had hit what off him and he never gave the guy the same pitch twice. He kept a mental book on batters. John Fulton who hated catching Jerry's crazy fast balls liked catching Tony who was always around the plate.

Maybe Tony was too much around the plate. Opposing batters could always count on getting a good ball to hit. With Jerry they were always a little tight and worried up there, but with Tony they were ready to swing. The McLeod Builders began first ball-hitting Tony.

Their first baseman, Jimmy Harris, a big guy, led off their half-inning by lining the first pitch at Jeff Bigler. Jeff caught it and then had to shout at the plate ump: "Can't make that a hit for them, can you, Ump?"

"Shut up, Bigler," I shouted, and we whipped the ball around.

John Fulton came out to talk to Tony about trying for the corners. If Tony didn't hit the corners, they'd knock that ball all over the park. Tony agreed. He was a scrappy little pitcher, and the best fielding pitcher in the league. It was like having another infielder out there.

Tony wound up and came down with his curve. Right over the heart of the plate. The batter timed it and slapped it over Danny Kohl's head at shortstop. Ned Franks charged in and I could see right away what he was up to. I hoped Dick Williams at second knew what was about to happen. Ned pretended to bobble the ball. The McLeod kid took a wide turn and decided to sprint for second. Ned whipped the ball on a line to Dick Williams. I held my breath. The throw was good. Dick who was a great outfielder but hadn't had much experience at second caught the ball, whirled, and put the tag on the runner. "Out," thumbed the bases ump.

Although it had worked, it was getting outs the hard way, and I chewed Ned out for it. It was one thing to work the fake bobble with Tony, our regular second baseman, but it was taking a chance with Dick.

"Aw," Dick said, "I can play second base as good as Tony."

"Yeah," I growled, "well, no more of that, Franks, or I'll beat your butt after the game."

Ned giggled, dumb enough to feel pleased with himself. It was hard to coach kids your own age. The only way you could get them to respect you was to wrestle them into the ground. I'd have to go to work on Ned this week.

At the mound John was talking to Tony again about the importance of throwing a few bad pitches. They were first pitch swinging because all his balls were over the heart of the plate. If we could only give Jerry a little of Tony's control and Tony a little of Jerry's great speed.

First pitch hitting was smart of McLeod's for another reason. It meant they weren't trying to place the ball into the empty space in right field. I've seen more teams beat themselves trying to put the ball where the other team was shorthanded. Major leaguers can do that, but not kids eleven years old. We ought to be swinging away and that's all.

John Fulton squatted down, gave Tony a signal, and then he moved his target off the plate. But I guess it was just impossible for old Tony to throw a bad pitch. This one came right down the middle and of course the kid was swinging. He hit a line shot between me and Danny. I dove for it and knocked it down. It took a lucky hop toward Danny who grabbed it and fired it over to first. Bigler gave it the big stretch. I thought maybe the McLeod kid had it beat, but the bases ump thumbed the out. I wondered if he was trying to make something up to us because of the plate ump. And I knew that if he was it would be a mistake because it would only get Mr. McLeod sore again and then old Bigler would get sore and someone would get tossed out of the game and it probably wouldn't be Mr. McLeod.

Sure enough, Mr. McLeod was protesting the call at first.

"Shut up, Bigler," I said, as we came trotting in.

Jeff grinned sweetly at me. "You don't hear me complaining, Jake."

"Well," Dick said, "it looks like we got one ump and they got the other ump."

"Only they got the balls and strikes ump," Ned said.
"It won't make any difference if we get some hits," I said.

"Suppose he starts calling them funny again?"

"Don't give him a chance. Hit the ball."

"I'm not swinging at bad pitches," Bigler said.

I squatted down alongside Jerry and chucked his chin up. "How you doin', man?"

He twisted away from me. "Cut it out, Jake."

I slapped the side of his head lightly. "We'll win this one for you, big fella. Who we got up, Mrs. Fulton?"

"Black, Jones—no, Jerry's out. Fulton, Bigler, Williams, Franks. . ."

"Jake, you were up last inning, you coach at third. Tony, get on first." That was Ned Franks, our ninth hitter, giving the orders. One thing I really liked about our club. Having no coach, we were all coaches.

Andy Black was first up. He was our clean-up hitter. A big easy-going guy with extra-sized muscles. Andy was a mild giant, but when stirred to wrath—man, look out.

Mr. McLeod took one look at Andy's size and began moving his outfielders back. A smart move. The only trouble with it was he didn't move them back far enough. Andy wasn't taking any chances on the plate ump, so when that first pitch came in, high and slow, around his chin, he stepped into it, and really socked it. It went way over the center fielder's head and rolled all the way to the ravine. Andy, running like a fullback with knees pumping high, was across home plate before the ball got back to the infield. We pounded our big man's back as he came trotting back to the bench, grinning shyly.

"Way to pound it," Bigler said. "That rat of an ump would have called it a foul if you hit it into left field."

"Shut up, Bigler," I said. "Swing a bat, you're up after Fulton."

Bigler never knew when he was inviting trouble. It would be nice to have a man coach to tell people like Bigler to shut up.

Little chunky John Fulton was up, chewing gum, swinging his bat, breaking his wrists. He swung a big bat and he was always tough up there. John had a good eye and always made contact with the ball. His trouble was his feet. He had big clodhopper feet, and it made him a very slow runner. John needed a double to get a single. I once actually saw John turn a home run into a double. His mother got so upset with him she threatened to chase him with a broomstick.

Pat McLeod kicked and threw a fast ball for a change. It wasn't much of a fast ball but there it was. It was around John's knees.

"Strike," the ump said.

"Shut up, Bigler," I said.

"Was that a bad call?" Mrs. Fulton asked.

"Not necessarily," I said.

Pat McLeod wound up and his next pitch was a curve right at John. He pulled away from it. "Strike two," the ump said.

John looked surprised.

"Shut up, Bigler," I said.

Jeff closed his mouth.

The McLeod infield began talking it up. Andy's home run had taken some of the spirit out of them, but now the ump was beefing them up again.

"Time, Ump," I said, and came in from the third-base coaching box. Johnny came out.

"How were those pitches?"

"I'm not so sure about the second pitch." He shrugged. "Maybe they were both strikes."

"You gotta protect the plate now."

"Yeah. I know."

"You gotta swing at anything you can reach."

He nodded, blowing a bubble out of his gum. Snap, it broke. He was cool, little John. Cool enough to carry out my idea.

"John, the third baseman's playing way back on the grass."

He shook his head. "I got two strikes on me, Jake."

"Lay it down fair and you're on."

John looked doubtful. Not doubtful about laying a bunt down fair, but doubtful about beating the throw to first. Here he was, the slowest runner on the club being asked to bunt with nobody on base and two strikes on him. It was the kind of daring play that could just work. But first I had to make John believe he could do it. In three years of playing in the Arborville Recreation League, he had never bunted his way on base once.

"All you got to do is tap it," I said. "He'll never even get to it. Heck, man, don't do it. You probably can't."

John blew his gum out. He was a battler. I knew then he'd give it a try.

"They're stalling again, Ump," Mr. McLeod shouted. "Make them play ball. A team without a coach. What can you expect from them? A circus."

"Shut up, Bigler," I said automatically, and Bigler shut his mouth.

John Fulton dug in at the plate. He gave the pitcher a tough look. He did not look as though he was going to bunt. And no one would be expecting a two-strike no-base runner bunt from the slowest runner in Arborville.

Pat came down with his pitch. A low curve. The best kind to bunt. John squared around and bunted it beautifully down the third-base line. The ball died in the tall grass. The third baseman, caught way out, didn't have a chance. He didn't even make a play on it, and old John galloped slowly to first base.

"Nice call, Jake," Jerry said.

I winked at him. Jerry was back in the game, at least as a spectator. They weren't able to break up our team when we lost our man coach, and they couldn't hurt us when they threw our best pitcher out, because part of him would stay in and pick up the rest of us.

Jeff Bigler, hot-tempered, loud-mouthed, stepped.

"Come on, Noisy," I shouted, "give it a rap."

Jeff was in many ways just the opposite of John Fulton. He had bad eyes (he wore glasses), but he could run like the wind. His older brother had been a state mile champ in high school, and Jeff was going to be even faster. We all knew his spring sport in high school would be track, not baseball. But right now he was a big part of our team. A noisy part, but he got on base a lot. Either through walks or dinky leg hits. Anything hit slow on the ground by Bigler was a sure base hit. And once he got on, he was a terror. He never got a good jump as a base stealer, because he had no baseball instincts at all, but he was so fast it didn't make any difference. Jeff would steal a base a pitch until he was home.

The third baseman moved in looking for the bunt. So did the first baseman. I clapped my hands and shouted to Jeff to swing away. I doubt that he heard me. The first pitch from Pat was a high fast ball, and the ump called it a ball, thank goodness. I hate to think what Bigler would have called him if he'd called that pitch a strike. I relaxed a little. It looked as though my threat to have Mrs. Fulton write down all unfair calls was working. It looked like we'd won that particular battle.

Pat's next pitch was a good curve, in for a strike. Then he threw one too low, and then Jeff with a mighty swing topped a dinky squibbler down to second.

Hustling hard, the second baseman made a nice pick up. He had an easy play at second because old John was only three-quarters of the way there, galloping slowly. But he chose to go to first instead. It was a smart move. Although you're always supposed to get the lead runner if you can, Bigler was just too fast to allow on base. He'd be a threat to steal his way all around. At second base, John was no threat at all. The throw to first just barely beat Jeff, but beat him it did. The bases ump, our friend, thumbed Jeff out.

And Jeff, the jackass, started screaming.

"Shut up, Bigler," I shouted.

But you could no more shut up Jeff Bigler than plug a geyser with your hand. He was jumping up and down telling the one good ump that he was blind as a bat.

Mr. McLeod was up off his bench telling the ump not to be afraid to throw Jeff out of the game. Tony Parker, our first-base coach, was trying to pull Jeff away from the ump, while Jimmy Harris, their big first baseman, was watching the whole thing and grinning from ear to ear. All this happening in a blur of noise when all of a sudden a loud warning shout went up from the McLeod parents in the stands. They were pointing. We all turned to see. Little old John Fulton, the slowest runner in Arborville, was trying to take advantage of the commotion by stealing third. Nobody had called "time."

The McLeod third baseman screamed for the ball, but Jimmy Harris never threw it. I guess the sight of Fulton stealing a base so shook him up he got paralyzed. As for John, even though there was no play on him at third, he slid in triumphantly in a cloud of dust.

"You!" Mr. McLeod screamed. "Get back on second."

"Stay where you are, John," I said softly.

"Time was called," Mr. McLeod shouted. "Get him back to second, Ump."

This was the time we needed a man coach.

"I didn't hear anyone call time," I said. "Did you, Ump?"

The bases ump didn't look happy about it, but he shook his head. "No," he said.

Mr. McLeod got red in the face. "I won't let you kids get away with this. Either that man goes back to second or—"

That was as far as he got. His mouth hung open, but no words came out. My mouth hung open, too. Everyone was staring at what was happening now. John Fulton got up, took a quick look around, and he was now chugging down the third-base line, heading for home. Like an old steam engine. Puff, chug, puff, chug, puff.

Jimmy Harris held onto the ball. He looked helplessly at Mr. McLeod and I knew what was going through his mind. If he threw the ball home it would be an admission that "time" had not been called. And the coach knew it too. Mr. McLeod was undecided. But I guess the sight of old John chugging home so slowly was too much for him. "Throw it, you idiot!" he roared.

Jimmy threw it. He threw it ten feet over the catcher's head. The ball rolled all the way to the backstop. That didn't prevent old John from arriving in style anyway. He slid in, just as though it were a close play. He slid in and dumped the flabbergasted catcher for good measure.

Mr. McLeod came storming onto the field. "If that runner doesn't get put back onto second," he said to the plate ump, "I'm going to pull my team out of this game. And you won't hear the end of this. I guarantee you'll both be through umping in this league."

"Hey, Mrs. Fulton," I said loudly, "will you write down

that the coach of that team is threatening both the umps unless they call the play his way."

The plate ump heard me. I guess he didn't know which to be scared of: Mrs. Fulton's report or Mr. McLeod's temper.

He decided to confer with the bases ump. Everyone crowded around them, including Mrs. Fulton and her paper and pencil.

The bases ump again said nobody called "time." The plate ump was reluctant but he finally said he didn't hear anyone call "time" either.

"That's it," Mr. McLeod said. "This circus is over. We're leaving. We shouldn't be playing a team without a coach in the first place. All right, McLeod Builders off the field."

I turned to the bases ump. "Do we win on a forfeit?"

The bases ump didn't look happy, but he shrugged and said: "I guess so."

"We win, gang," I shouted, and our guys began jumping up and down. We pounded the hero of the game— old John Fulton. We picked Jerry up and hugged him as though he'd pitched a no-hitter for nine innings. We pounded Tony and climbed all over a grinning Andy Black. The only one not happy was our "coach." She was staring grimly at her son's dirty uniform.

"Why are you the only one to get his uniform messed up?" she asked.

"Aw, Ma," John said.

The guys laughed, and I grinned, thinking how my Uncle Lenny didn't give a hoot whether my uniform was black or white. There was lots of advantages in being taken care of by a rock and roll musician who doesn't give a hoot.

Of course, I'd like to go home and tell him about this incredible victory, but he wouldn't be there. So while all the other guys on the team went home to tell their folks about this crazy victory, I went home to go over it alone.

I'm pretty good at doing things alone.

5.

Savor. The word is "savor." S-A-V-O-R. It's a fancy word I got from my Uncle Lenny one night. He was home on a Sunday night listening over and over to a record, like nothing else was important. It was one of his own records, too. (How much of a showboat can a guy be?) An atom bomb could have gone off and he wouldn't have heard it.

"What're you doing?" I asked him for the fourth time.

"I'm savorin', Jake," he said. "Just savorin'."

"What's that mean?"

He looked up at me. "You are one big ignoramus, boy."

"I know that, but how'm I gonna learn if I don't ask questions?"

Lenny sighed. He started the record over again. "Savor means lickin' your lips and enjoyin'. Like my lead guitar part on that record. Listen to it."

"Can you savor other stuff besides your own lead guitar?" Lenny threw a pillow at my head. But I ducked under it. He didn't have as good an arm as he used to have.

My turn to start this "savorin' " business came the night after the forfeit victory over the McLeod Builders. That night I made myself some hot dogs and apple sauce and had a glass of iced coffee and turned on the TV. I sat up half the night with the TV but not really watching it. I just sat there savorin' that crazy ball game. And everytime I saw old John Fulton come tearing up those basepaths, with those big heavy clodhopper feet of his, I started laugh-in' and savorin' at the same time.

It was a great victory, and I figured it would last me all my life.

I was wrong. It didn't even last twenty-four hours.

The next morning I got up late. Our old alarm clock doesn't work anymore and it was only Lenny's snoring that woke me up. He and I share a bed, which is like sharing a bed with a bear. Lenny's over six foot three and over two hundred pounds. He's quiet enough when he gets back from Detroit. I mean, he doesn't wake me when's he's awake, but it's after he falls asleep that he starts taking over the bed. Sometimes I have to kick him real hard to move him back to his side of the bed.

School is supposed to start at eight thirty. To get there on time I should leave by eight fifteen. But it was after eight when I woke.. With Lenny's snores filling the apartment, I hustled in to make my breakfast: a fried egg, bread, and a cup of instant coffee. The fry pan hadn't been cleaned since two days ago. Lenny was supposed to clean it but I guess he forgot.

I ran it under cold water and wiped the grease off with a paper towel. Then I put some bacon fat in and fried me an egg. I boiled water for the coffee. Lenny's always kidding me that if I don't make the major leagues, I can always get a job as a short-order cook.

After I ate, I left Lenny the pan and dishes to wash and hustled off to school. Only fifteen minutes late by the big clock in the corridor, but when I saw old Atwell's face as I slipped into the classroom, I knew I was in trouble.

Mrs. Atwell is OK as a teacher. She doesn't bug me any more than other guys, but this morning she looked like she'd finally had it with me. Maybe she'd had a fight with her husband. You can't tell about adults. Sometimes you do someting bad and they smile and you know they're thinking "it's just kids," but the next day you do the exact same thing and they're all over you. Probably because they had a fight with their husband or wife. That's one reason I'm glad Lenny's not married. Everything that happens between him and me is really between him and me. I'm not much worried about anyone marrying my uncle either. Who in their right mind would marry a big guitar-playing ex-basketball player who never washes the fry pan?

Mrs. Atwell doesn't say a thing till I'm in my seat. Then she says the most unnecessary thing in the world: "Jake, you're late again."

"Yeah, I know." The whole class bursts into laughter, like I've said something witty. Even Dick Williams and Danny Kohl from the team are laughing.

That really gets old Atwell mad. Her lips tighten. Here comes the hassle, I think glumly.

"Jake, you had better go down to Miss Bradsbury's office."

"OK," I say and get up. And the idiots in the class laugh again. Like everything I say or do is funny. If I hiccuped,

I'd probably have them rolling on the floor. I give them my dirty look and go downstairs.

Nobody likes to go down to old Raspberry's office. She's a tough old lady with dyed red hair. Lenny had her as a teacher right here in Sampson School about a hundred years ago and he told me he was scared stiff of her then, and probably still is now. Besides that fake red hair, she's got thick glasses and a jaw that looks like it could break stones inside it. I've told kids she looks like something out of the late late show on TV, but they don't know what the late late show is.

Tony Parker, our second baseman, is in the outer office when I get there.

"Man, what're you doing here?"

"Gettin' supplies," he says. 'What about you?"

"Gettin' chewed out."

"Yeah? Tough." Tony's all sympathy. "You hear about them meeting this morning?"

"Who's meeting?"

"Mr. McLeod and the league president—that Fredericks guy."

"No. What about?"

"McLeod wants Fredericks to take our forfeit victory away from us."

"He can't do that. We won it. The umps said we won it."

"Maybe so. But Ned Franks heard from someone on the McLeod team that's what's happening. We're gonna meet at the flagpole before lunch."

"Listen, they—"

I was going to say they couldn't change their minds like that—it wasn't baseball, when the door to old Raspberry's office opened and there was old Raspberry herself, big as Lenny almost, fixing us with a steely look. Tony grabbed his supplies and scooted out faster than he ever got a jump in a ball game. There's our coach, I thought, trying not to grin, old Raspberry. That McLeod guy wouldn't yell at her OK.

"Jake," she said in a deep voice.

"Yes, ma'am."

"I've been waiting for you. Come in."

"Yes, ma'am."

I go in. A big old hairy office with lots of pictures on the walls of classes that have graduated from Sampson School for the past hundred years. Lenny's up there somewhere. So's my mom. But I don't look. I look down at my sneakers, like I'm scared. I'm not really scared. There's nothing and no one in the world I'm scared of. I'm not bragging. I'm just humbly stating a fact.

"Sit down there, Jake."

I sat down in a fat red leather chair. I went way, way down, till I was pretty small down there and she was enormous up there, and I knew she'd done that on purpose. If she wanted to grab me and sock me, there was no way I could get up fast enough.

"Jake, this is the third time you've been late this week. Is that right?"

"I guess so."

"Don't you know?"

"Yes, ma'am."

"Do you dislike school, Jake?"

I hadn't been expecting that question. "I . . . no," I said truthfully. "School's all right."

"Then why are you late?"

"My alarm clock don't work."

"Why not?"

"'Cause it's busted."

"How long has it been busted?"

I looked up at the ceiling as though I were trying to figure it out. Fact was: I was trying to figure out the right answer. The right answer isn't always the truthful answer. It's the answer that keeps adults off balance. It's like a boxing match with adults. Keep moving and they move with you and then they forget what the whole thing was about in the first place.

"I think it was busted when we bought it. We're gonna take it back to the store. You think they'll give us a new one, Miss Bradsbury?"

She doesn't answer. She's staring at me grimly. Too tough, I think.

"I've got an extra alarm clock, Jake. Would you like it?"

"Yes, ma'am. I'd like it. But my Uncle Lenny wouldn't."

"Why not?"

"He doesn't like me taking gifts."

"Then tell your uncle to get that clock fixed."

"It can't be fixed, Miss Bradsbury. It's broke from the bottom up, if you know what I mean."

"I don't."

Fact was: I didn't either. But we were off the track. In conversations like this you got to run out of the baseline if you want to get home safe.

"Anyway, Uncle Lenny says he's got an alarm clock in his head. All I got to do is tell him what time I want to get up and he sets the screw in his head and wakes me."

"What happened this morning?"

"He forgot to set the screw."

She doesn't smile. "Jake, your uncle works nights in Detroit, doesn't he?"

A little alarm goes off inside me. "Yes, ma'am. He rehearses there every night. He's lead guitar."

She doesn't go for the music bit.

"What time does he leave for Detroit?"

"About six."

"What time did you get home from your ball game yesterday?"

How'd she know we had a ball game? Talk about doing your homework!

"About seven thirty."

"So you didn't see him last night, did you?"

I shook my head, thinking quick how to get off the Uncle Lenny-and-me topic. It was a bad one. No good could come of it. People were always trying to bust us up. I was wrong a few minutes ago when I said I wasn't scared of anything. That's the one thing I am scared of. Me and Lenny busting up, and me being shipped off to some foster home or something. They've been threatening to do that to us since we started living together.

Lenny is my mom's younger brother. When my father and mother busted up, me and my ma moved in with Lenny. Then two years ago, my mom's mother in West Virginia got sick and my ma went down there to take care of her and she's never come back since. I'm pretty sure she got married down there and is starting another family and don't want me around to remind her of the past. I don't want to go down there either. I like it in Arborville; I like playing ball here; I like living with Lenny. I'm on my own. No one bugging me, no hassles with older folks. And just being around Lenny is a real treat. He's a dude. Just walking down the street with him is an education. He was a big basketball and football player at Arborville High, and then he went on and played basketball for the University. Everyone in town knows him. After he finished at the University, he played semipro baseball for a while and then he became a rock and roll musician. You don't become that really. I mean, he always played the guitar, but then he really started working at it. Now he's in this rock group from Arborville, but the trouble is they can't find a place to rehearse here in town so they go into Detroit every night to jam there. They cut records in Detroit and play in a night club there on the weekends. Just about the only times Lenny and I see each other is at noon when I'm coming home for lunch and he's getting up for breakfast. Lenny's all the father and mother I'll ever need. He buys good food and we have fun. I got the best life going I know.

But there's old Raspberry, red hair, big-jawed, thick glasses, looking down at me grimly. I know what she's going to say, and I try to keep the panic down.

"I think, Jake, I'll have to ask your uncle to pay me a visit."

"He's pretty busy, ma'am," I say, calmer than I feel.

"I know he is. But if he's going to become your guardian he'll have to start acting like one. There's a real question, Jake, whether an eleven-year-old boy can live a normal life with an uncle who is out of town most of the time. Is your uncle home now?"

"Please don't call him. He's sleeping now."

"Jake, you've been late three times this week, when you're in class Mrs. Atwell tells me you're half asleep. I understand you're the only child in this school who sees the late late show regularly." Her voice softened. "Jake, you're a tough little boy. I know. And everyone likes you, which I find strange. But nobody eleven years old is tough enough or has enough friends to get through life alone. You go back to class now and stay awake in class."

"I will, Miss Bradsbury. Please don't wake up my uncle."

"Go back to class, Jake."

I went.

Danny Kohl, our shortstop, sits three seats from me. Seeing him, I forget about old Raspberry and remember what Tony Parker said about their trying to take our forfeit victory away from us. I whip a note off to Danny asking him what he knows about it. Old Atwell catches us and chews us both out, me especially, and that's it for the morning. I'm batting zero.

Lunchtime: the school lets out with a whoop and a holler. Danny and Dick and I hustle out to the flagpole for our team meeting. Ned's in the middle telling the guys that the Owens kid who plays right field for the McLeod Builders told him that Mr. McLeod was meeting this morning with Mr. Fredericks, the league president, to talk him into making us play that game over.

Jeff Bigler is hopping mad as usual. They all look at me for what to do.

"John, did they tell your mother about this meeting?"

"She didn't tell me."

"Then let's forget it. She's our coach. They got to tell her. They got to have her in on any meeting like that. That kid from the Builders has got it all mixed up. Who're we playing tomorrow?"

"Baer Machine. At Vets Park."

"What time?"

"Quarter to six."

"Can Jerry pitch the whole game?"

"We'll worry about that tomorrow. You guys be down there by five fifteen. Anyone who's late I'm gonna separate their head from their body. And no more hassles with the other team. You hear me, Bigler?"

"What're you picking on me for, Jake?"

"I'm telling you straight, all of you. No more hassling. I don't care how rotten the umps are. We play baseball and beat them that way. Forfeit's no way to win anyway. We're in first place and that's where we're gonna stay."

"How about a practice today, Jake?"

"You guys want to practice?"

"Yeah. Sure. Why not?"

I tried not to grin. I was proud of these guys. We lived to play baseball. We didn't need an adult male coach. All we needed was to be left alone to do our thing: playing baseball. Nobody was going to beat the Print-Alls in the Arborville Eleven-Year-Old League.

"OK. Meet at the Park. Three forty-five at diamond two."

"You think we ought to reserve it, Jake?" Dick asked.

"Don't worry about that. We'll kick off anyone who's on it."

Old Jerry laughs. "You sure are one tough guy, Jake."

I glare at him, and they all break up and I laugh, too. Fact is: though I am tough, I'm thinking, too. The junior high kids who are bigger than us don't get out of school till three forty-five. That leaves only the sixth graders, and there isn't a sixth grader in all of Arborville I can't handle.

"Bigler, you help Fulton with the equipment bag. Three forty-five, diamond two. See you guys."

I had to hustle home. They have mothers making their lunches, but I got to make my own. On the way, I wondered if old Raspberry had called Lenny. I sure hoped not.

6.

LENNY AND I SHARE ONE-HALF OF A ONE-STORY HOUSE. Mr. and Mrs. Witherspoon live in the other half. They're an old couple whose kids are grown up and married. Once in a while they pay me to mow the grass on their side of the house, but ever since our weeds started crawling onto their lawn, they've been kind of sore at me and Lenny. Once in a while I'm out of food, I'll knock on their door and Mrs. Witherspoon will feel sorry for me and give me a sandwich. Today, I had the crazy idea I ought to do just that. Pretend we were out of food so I wouldn't have to face Lenny, if he was awake.

I hesitated on the front porch between our door and the Witherspoons', when old Lenny's voice floated through the open window.

"This way, Jake," he said.

That was it. Old Raspberry had called and woken him. Well, the best defense is a good offense.

"Hey, man," I said, walking in, "out of the way, I got to make myself lunch."

Lenny was at the kitchen table smoking a cigarette over a cup of coffee, wearing his sunglasses. That was the bad sign. Those dark glasses always went on before we hassled. He didn't want me to know what he was thinking. Like, I figure, sometimes he chews me out because he thinks he's supposed to, but deep down he doesn't care.

I wasn't sure what it was going to be right now, but I wasn't taking any chances. I pretended to ignore him while I hustled a lunch out of the refrigerator. Got the water into a pot for some coffee, and got bread out of the breadbox.

"Hey, man," I said, "we're short on bread."

Lenny didn't answer. Another bad sign.

"We're long on peanut butter," I said, more cheerfully than I felt. Fact is: I like peanut butter. It's got lots of protein which is good for ball players. I spread it on the last of the bread. Then I got out the jar of instant coffee, almost down to the bottom.

"Short on coffee, Lenny," I said.

He didn't say a thing. Just sat there like a huge cat, smoke curling around his ears. I didn't like it one bit, but I kept hustling and bustling around the kitchen.

Finally Lenny spoke: "Don't you drink milk anymore, Jake?"

Surprised, I looked at him: "Milk cuts down your wind. Don't you know that?"

"That so?" His voice was amused. "Who told you that, old Jake?"

"Mickey Mason."

"Mickey Mason ... who's he?"

"He plays for the University. Shortstop."

"That right? A college ball player?"

"Yeah. Good, too."

"How do you come to know a college ball player, Jake?"

"Heck, man, I go down to Ferry Field and shag balls for them sometimes."

"That right?"

"Uh huh."

"You do that during school or afterward?"

"Now what kind of thing is that to ask, Lenny? I go to school. I do it after school."

Old Raspberry had got to him. Here it was coming. I concentrated on pouring the hot water into the coffee, stirring it slowly. Then I got some milk and poured a little in. Then two teaspoons of sugar.

All the while I know Lenny's watching me, as though he's never seen a human being make a cup of coffee before.

When I'm done, I bite into the sandwich and sip the coffee. There's a faint amused smile on Lenny's face. I'd like to bust him one.

"You're pretty set on being a ball player," he says.

"I might take a shot at it," I say.

"Who's the lucky team gonna be? Tigers or White Sox?"

"Maybe the Indians. I hear they need third basemen."

Lenny laughs. He doesn't want to laugh, he wants to give me hell and a spanking, too, but he's got to laugh. "Jake, you're too much."

I don't smile. I blow on my coffee. I eat my sandwich. He knows I'm defensing him but he doesn't know what to do about it yet. And him an old basketball player.

He goes back to the coffee front.

"Didn't anybody ever tell you coffee stunts a kid's growth?"

"No."

"It does, Jake. That's a fact."

"How come Wilt Chamberlain's been drinking it since he was four years old?"

For a second old Lenny was fazed, then he shakes his head: "How come you're such a bad liar?"

"I'm not a liar. I read it in a sports magazine."

"You didn't read a thing anywhere. You don't even know how to read."

"Are you mocking me, man? I can read the back of the coffee can from here. It says—"

"Be quiet, Jake."

"You said I couldn't—"

"I wanna know how many times you been late to school this week."

He'd finally got there. I felt like I ought to congratulate him, but now I knew I had to go carefully. It was time to stop clowning around. Time for the truth. If old Raspberry had got to him, and why else would he be awake and sore right now, then he knew.

"Three times."

"Didn't I give you money to buy a new alarm clock last week?"

"Yeah."

"What did you do with that money, Jake?"

"I bought a bat."

"You bought a bat?" He repeated it like he couldn't

believe it.

I grinned. "Aw, Lenny, if you had three bucks and went into a store and saw a Tony Oliva bat and a stupid-looking alarm clock. Which would you buy?"

Lenny looked grave. He tapped his cigarette into the ash tray. "I guess when you put it that way, I'd have bought the bat."

"That's what I did."

"But then I'd be prepared to accept the consequences, Jake."

"What consequences?"

"This consequence."

He was quick. I'll say that for him. Old Lenny's twenty-four years old, but he's still got the quickest hands in Arborville. One of those quick hands sneaked out and pulled me across the table.

"Hey, what're you doing? You're getting my shirt dirty."

My chest scraped the table and I got peanut butter all over my shirt.

The next thing I knew I was up in the air, like a sack of potatoes, flipped, and then I was across Lenny's knee and his big hand was coming down on my rump.

"Hey, man, cut it out."

I punched him, but it was like punching a brick wall. Smack, smack . . . his big hand came down. It didn't hurt. It was just . . . humiliating.

When he was done, he let me go.

"Listen to me, Jake," he said softly, and I realized for the first time how mad he was, "that spanking didn't hurt you none, and it hurts me more than it hurts you. But I'm going to tell you something that may hurt. Miss Bradsbury doesn't think you ought to go on living with me. They're gonna break us up."

"They can't do that."

My rump didn't hurt anymore.

"Why can't they? I'm not your legal guardian. They can put you in a foster home faster than you think if they don't think I'm bringing you up right."

"You're bringing me up great." I sat down, and then got up again. My rump was tender.

"I'm bringing you up rotten. You're drinking coffee, watching TV to three in the morning, late to school, asleep in class ... all you care about is baseball." He leaned forward. "I know one solution I can start on right now."

"What's that?" I asked suspiciously.

"Yank you off that baseball team of yours."

"You can't do that."

"Are you telling me I can't make you quit playing baseball?"

"That's just what I'm telling you."

I doubled my hands into fists and glared at him.

"OK," Lenny said softly, "you are finished with baseball, Jake."

I spat and said two words to him which I've never said to an adult before. Lenny's reaction was immediate and quick. But this time I was ready. I ducked, swung at him, missed, but knocked over a chair. Lenny was coming on quick and he tripped over the chair. He threw the chair to one side and he was coming after me hard and mad now. It wouldn't just be a rump spanking this time. I turned and ran for the living room and the front door. He was three steps behind me.

The front screen door was shut. I'd never get it unlatched in time. He'd collar me first. There was only one thing to do now, and I didn't hesitate.

I dove through the window screen, hands, head, and the rest of me… I could feel the metal wires scrape my face, my elbows, but I was through, all of me was through, and I was lying head down on the front porch. I jumped up, ready to take off down the block. But there was no movement inside the house. Lenny wasn't coming after me.

He was standing inside, on the other side of the biggest hole you ever saw in any screen, his sunglasses off, peering through the hole at me.

"You all right, Jake?" he asked softly.

"Yeah," I growled.

He didn't say a thing. Me neither. Then he grinned; he grinned all over his big plug-ugly face. I started grinning, too. We stood there like a couple of lunatics grinning at each other through the hole in the screen.

Then he unlatched the door and came out. He wasn't mad anymore. I wasn't scared anymore. He looked me over to see if I was bleeding anywere. When he saw I wasn't, he held out an open palm like the ball players do and I slapped it.

"Come in, I'll wash you off."

"I'm OK."

"Don't be so damn hard-nosed all the time."

We stopped. The other front door opened and there were Mr. and Mrs. Witherspoon staring at us with alarm.

Mr. Witherspoon cleared his throat. "Are you boys all right?"

"We're fine, Mr. Witherspoon," Lenny said, smiling. "Old Jake decided to test the living-room screen."

Mr. Witherspoon came out and carefully examined the hole in the screen. "The boy done a right fine job," he said.

Later I found out from some kid who hangs around the principal's office that old Raspberry had woke up Lenny and told him that unless I straightened out she was going to speak with the social workers about my living with a twenty-four-year-old uncle who didn't care what happened to me.

And that was sure the wrong way to talk to my Uncle Lenny because even if he thought we ought to split, which he thought lots of times—for his sake as well as mine—even if he thought that he wouldn't have done it just because some tough old bat of a principal was telling him he had to do it.

That just put his old back up. Raspberry couldn't have done me more of a favor than by threatening him. Lenny just didn't like to be pushed around. My big worry was that some day one of those music cats he played with was going to drag him off to Chicago or New York, or that he'd meet a girl and get soupy enough to marry her and she wouldn't want me around.

But as long as old Raspberry kept chewing him out, she was doing me a favor. At least, that's how I figured the situation.

7.

It was my day to be late for everything. In the morning I was late for school because I had no alarm clock. In the afternoon I was late for baseball practice because I had to go buy one. I also had to buy a half gallon of milk. Milk plus a clock meant no more hassling about my playing baseball.

By the time I got to Sampson Park it was after three forty-five and I couldn't see any of the Print-Alls around. A bunch of little kids—third and fourth graders—were playing on diamond two.

"You guys see the Print-Alls?" I asked them.

"They went over to John Fulton's house, Jake," a kid answered me. "They said to tell you that."

I gave the kid my hard look. "Did we let you punks take over our diamond?"

"Naw," the kid said with a giggle, "we pushed you off."

That's the kind of blather little kids give you these days. I hustled across the park, past the tennis courts—a sissy game if ever there was one—and over to John Fulton's house. Sure enough, a whole bunch of bikes were parked on the grass in front, and through their picture window I could see the guys in the living room. One of them waved at me.

Jeff Bigler opened the door. "Where've you been?"

"Buying milk and an alarm clock."

He looked at me as though I were nuts.

The guys were all over the living room, on the floor, on chairs, on the couch, and all over were bats, gloves, balls, and caps. Mrs. Fulton was sitting there, too, not looking very happy about the situation.

"What gives?" I asked.

"We're waiting for the league president to get here," Dick Williams said.

"Sit down, Jake," Mrs. Fulton said. "I had to call a team meeting right away."

"He's coming over to tell us we didn't win yesterday's game," Jeff said.

"Now you don't know that, Jeff," Mrs. Fulton said.

"Why else would he want to meet?"

"I don't know," she admitted.

I grinned. "You're not going to let him take away our victory, are you, Mrs. Fulton?"

"Of course not," she said. "He's only the president of the Arborville Recreation Baseball League; I'm the coach of the Print-Alls."

"Aw, Ma," John Fulton said, embarrassed.

A couple of guys laughed, but we all had the feeling that this meeting with Mr. Fredericks was going to bring us out on the short end of the stick. And maybe that was part of the price you paid for choosing a lady coach. You picked her because you had to have an adult, then you liked it because it meant not having a coach at all, but not having a coach at all also meant nobody to stick up for you when the other adults landed heavy on you. We needed a man coach right now more than ever.

"That looks like Mr. Fredericks."

We all looked out the window. A gray-haired man was coming up the walk.

"He looks mean."

"He doesn't look anything of the sort," Mrs. Fulton said. "I'll give you boys one bit of free advice: be polite."

"Yeah, Bigler."

"Why me? I'm polite."

"If you're so polite, why don't you open the door for the guy?" Jerry asked.

"Aw, nuts," Bigler said, but he opened the door and Mr. Fredericks came in. We'd all seen him at games from time to time. He looked like an old ball player. He also had that straight look that told you he played by the rules, and he didn't like the idea of a lady coach. He greeted Mrs. Fulton politely, and said, "Hello, boys," to us and then he went into his little speech.

"I know you're wondering why I've asked to meet with all of you rather than just with Mrs. Fulton."

I was interested that he didn't say "your coach." Just Mrs. Fulton.

"The reason I've asked to meet with all of you is simply, and with all due respect to Mrs. Fulton, you are a team playing without a coach. You know, I believe, that at the beginning of the season, when it became evident that Mr. Parker couldn't coach you, the suggestion was made that your team be broken up and the players go to other teams."

"I bet I know who suggested it," Bigler said. "That guy McLeod."

"Shut up, Bigler," I said.

"As a matter of fact, Son," Mr. Fredericks said, "you wouldn't have been the only team breaking up. Arborville Recreation League baseball is like a pyramid. Wide at the bottom and getting smaller on top. We have well over five hundred kids playing in the nine-year-old league, about four fifty in the ten-year-old league, less than three hundred in the eleven-year-old league. And when you get up to the fifteen- and sixteen-year-old leagues, you only have about one hundred players. Every year the baseball gets a little tougher and teams lose players and teams have to be broken up. Sponsors drop out, and so do coaches. It's my own opinion that with only nine players on their roster, and no coach, the Print-Alls should have been broken up."

"What's wrong with nine guys?" Jeff asked. "That's all you need to play ball."

"What happens when one of you goes on vacation?"

"Nobody goes on vacation till the season's over," I said.

"Suppose someone gets sick?"

"He plays."

Mr. Fredericks smiled. He thought I was joking.

"All right," he said, "you're a tough bunch of dedicated ball players and you want to stick together and all of that is to your credit. But the fact you can't get away from is that you don't have a coach. You got Mrs. Fulton and

I believe we made a mistake in letting you do that. But Mrs. Fulton knows and I know and you know that you're really coaching yourselves, and this isn't so bad either unless something happens like your game yesterday with the McLeod Builders."

"They forfeited to us," Jeff said. "Not us to them."

"I know what happened," Mr. Fredericks said patiently. "I've talked with both umpires and I had a long talk with Mr. McLeod this morning. I'm not going to say I approve of his action yesterday, because I don't, and I told him so. But I can tell you boys that as a former coach myself I can share his frustration at not having a coach across the diamond he could talk things out with. Which one of you is Jake Wrather?"

Silence. Everyone looked at me, and so did Mr. Fredericks.

"Mr. McLeod tells me you run your team, Jake."

"I play third," I grunted.

"Yes, he mentioned that, too. He said you play a tough third base. When one of his players slid into third you put a hard tag on his head, dazing the boy for a second."

"He was sliding in headfirst. Where did you want me to tag him? On his ankles?"

"I'm not saying you didn't tag him in the right place, I'm just saying the opposing coach thought you tagged him hard enough to hurt him. When he went to protest to your coach, there was no coach. There was no one for him to talk with. What he did yesterday, pulling his team off the field, was in my opinion, a mistake. However, I can understand why he thought he had to do it. That was the first time anything like that has ever happened in our city. I don't think it would have happened if you boys had had a male coach there. Therefore, I've made the decision, which is a final one, to wash out yesterday's game, and reschedule it for Saturday morning at ten at Veterans Park. . . ."

That was as far as he got. Everyone started protesting at once. Mrs. Fulton tried to hush us up, but we wouldn't shut up, and from the amused look on Mr. Fredericks' face, I knew we were proving his point: Mrs. Fulton couldn't control us, and we couldn't control ourselves.

I banged my hand down on the coffee table. "Shut up," I shouted.

Everyone shut up. My hand hurt, but I didn't show it. I looked at Mr. Fredericks. "What else is there?" I said.

He looked at me and nodded as though something were clicking in his mind. "How did you know there was going to be something else?"

"I'm guessing."

"You've guessed correctly. I want you boys to get yourselves a man coach at each game. If you don't, you'll have to forfeit each game."

We all looked at each other. A man coach for each game. It was impossible. We'd been through the search for a coach already. There were no man coaches around. Forfeit each game. That was the end of the Print-Alls. They couldn't break us up by a direct order, but they could make us forfeit each game which was the same thing as breaking up.

No one said a thing. I guess we were all too stunned to protest. The season was suddenly ending, right there in the Fulton living room.

Finally, Bigler said in a small voice: "But we've got a game tomorrow afternoon against Baer Machine."

"Get a coach for tomorrow afternoon," Mr. Fredericks said.

"And Saturday morning?" Danny Kohl asked softly.

"Get a coach for Saturday morning."

"Does it have to be the same coach?" Ned asked.

"No. But it's got to be a man. It would be better if you had one coach for the rest of the season, like all the teams, but that may be asking too much. So what we're asking is for you to get a man coach down to each game."

Mr. Fredericks stood up. He turned to Mrs. Fulton. "Thank you for letting me come over and talk with the boys."

"Yeah, thanks," Bigler said bitterly.

"Shut up, Bigler," I said automatically, trying to figure a way out of this.

Dick Williams who had a strange sense of humor said: "How'd you like to coach us, Mr. Fredericks?"

Mr. Fredericks laughed. "It would be a real challenge, but hardly a proper duty for the league president. Goodbye, boys, I'm sorry about all of this, but in the long run it will be for your own good."

And with those cheerful words he left.

"Good-bye," Bigler said, "you rat."

"Now, Jeff," Mrs. Fulton said, "that wasn't necessary, was it?"

"I could have said something worse," Bigler said.

"Like what?" Dick Williams asked, grinning.

"Shut up, both of you," I growled. "We're in a real jam, and you're making jokes."

"Listen, Jake," Bigler said, "I'm sick of taking orders from you. Who do you think you are anyway?"

"Shut up, Jeff," Andy Black said quietly, and Jeff gaped at big old Andy and shut up. Andy turned to me. "What'll we do, Jake?"

"Find ourselves a coach. What else can we do?" "By a quarter to six tomorrow? You're kidding."

"Dick, what about your dad?"

Dick shook his head. We'd been through all this before. Dick's dad coached his older brother's team.

"What about your older brother?"

"His game's the same time as ours."

"John?"

John looked at his mother who shook her head. John's father was a salesman who wasn't home very often. "Danny?"

"My dad don't know anything about baseball." "We can teach him."

"Are you kidding? Nobody can teach my dad anything."

"Ned?"

"He doesn't have the time. I've asked him twenty times already."

I looked at Andy Black. Andy's father was a possibility.

He used to be a ball player. Once in the park I'd seen him hitting mile-high fungoes out to Andy and his brothers.

Andy shook his head. "He ain't feeling so good these days, Jake."

That left Jerry Jones and me. But we're both in the same boat. No father. Jerry's got a mother, three brothers, two sisters. And I got … Lenny.

"What about Lenny?" Bigler asked.

"He can't coach. He's a musician."

"He's a ball player. Ask him."

"When? He's in Detroit all the time. He goes to Detroit every afternoon around six to rehearse with his band. He doesn't get home till after midnight."

"Maybe he could stay around tomorrow and coach us, and maybe for Saturday we could find someone else."

"Forget it," I said. I knew Lenny. If I was tough, so was Lenny. And being an ex-ball player himself, he didn't think ball playing was all that important. In my experience it was those fathers who hadn't made it themselves playing ball who always wanted to coach and push their kids. Lenny had been one of Arborville's most famous athletes; so naturally, he wasn't impressed by my wanting to play ball. And his music had to come first. Heck, I couldn't blame him for that.

"Forget it and forfeit it," Bigler said bitterly. "Come on, Jake. Ask your uncle."

"No, man."

Why not?"

"Because it won't do any good. He gets enough trouble

from me without getting mixed up with kids' baseball."

I hoped they'd understand what I meant by that. But how could they? They all led normal lives with mothers and fathers and regular meals and stuff. How could they understand the crazy kind of life Lenny and I had. How could they understand how unfair it was for someone like Lenny to have to be a father and mother to me, and now they wanted him to be a baseball coach, too. Lenny wanted to be only one thing: a musician. Maybe the greatest musician in the world. No cat ever became a great musician by coaching kids' baseball.

"Forget it. He goes to Detroit every night."

"What happens tomorrow?" Tony asked.

No one had the answer for that. We all felt so depressed that when the meeting broke up, we didn't have the heart to go back to the park and practice.

What's the point in practicing anyway when they won't let you play real games?

8.

"If that man isn't in the batter's box by the time I count to three," the ump shouted, "this game is forfeited."

My hands were sweating and the bat was so heavy I couldn't pick it up.

"One," he called out.

I grabbed the bat with both hands and tugged.

"Two," he said.

"Help, Lenny," I screamed.

"Three!"

Darriinnnnnnnnnnnnnnnnnnng!

Lenny groaned. "What's the matter?"

I opened my eyes. I sighed with relief and turned off the alarm. "That's the new clock."

"Oh," he said, and went back to sleep.

I just lay there, thankful at being wakened from the nightmare of a bat too heavy to pick up and the umpire threatening to forfeit our game unless I picked the bat up.

That was the worst dream I ever had in my life.

I got up out of bed and pulled up the window shade. A cloudy gray day. It looked like it might rain. If only it would rain. We'd have an extra day in which to look for a coach.

I made breakfast and that included milk and with

Lenny's snores still ringing in my ears, I went off to school. It began to sprinkle. Rain harder, I prayed. Rain real hard and wash out our game.

I'd never before prayed for a rained-out game.

It only went on sprinkling, and when I got to school there were the usual soccer games going on. It had been a long time since I'd got to school early enough to take part in a soccer game. I wasn't very good at the sport. Sometimes I kicked a kid instead of the ball and sometimes the kid I kicked would get mad and want to scuffle. So we'd scuffle and word would get out that Jake Wrather was a dirty soccer player, when all I was was an awful soccer player. But I was pretty good at the scuffling part. Fact was: I liked the scuffling part.

Danny Kohl was in one of the games and he was fun to watch. Quick and agile, he anticipated the flow of the game. I watched him give a pass, and receive it right back and take it down the field to score. He was a natural athlete, good at any sport. I was good at only one sport: baseball. If I didn't make it in baseball, I was through.

The first bell rang and the game broke up. Ned Franks came up behind me.

"Hey, Jake, you're on time today."

"What's wrong with that?"

"Hey, don't get mad. I've never seen you on time." Ned looked up at the sky. "You think it'll rain harder than this?"

"I hope so."

"Me, too. Give us more time to find a coach."

I knew then that it would be on all the Print-Alls' minds. Pray for rain and search for a coach.

Inside the school we met Jeff Bigler looking gloomy. Ned slapped him hard on the back. That usually got Jeff sore, but he was too sad to get sore. Jeff said: "The rules say you got to show up with a full team even if it is raining. The ump can call a postponement if it's raining, but if one team doesn't have a coach and a team, he can also call it a forfeit."

"Is that right, Jake?"

I wasn't sure, but it was one of those things that sound so stupid you know it's got to be right. And I could remember the past two years we always showed up at ball diamonds in the rain and the two coaches always shook hands and discussed the weather situation with the umps. Only an ump could call a game off. Though sometimes they announced postponements over the local radio station. But then it had to be raining real hard for hours ahead of time. Not sprinkling like this.

"So you see," Jeff said, "even if it is raining, we got to get ourselves a coach."

"What'll we do, Jake?" Ned asked, as we walked down the hall to our classroom. We stopped at his locker while he put his lunch in it.

"I don't know. I'll think of something."

By the time Ned had put his lunch away and we were almost at our room I thought of it. We'd get down to Vets Park early and find some adult who'd pretend to be our coach for a couple of minutes, just long enough to shake hands with the Baer Machine coach and agree with the umps that the game ought to be called. There had to be an old guy down at Vets Park.

Ned brightened immediately when I told him my plan. "Jake, I've seen lots of old guys hanging around the park shelter playing cards."

Good old Ned. He walked into the class whistling as if all our problems were over. I just shook my head. It was a good idea because it was the only idea, but old Ned was too thick to see that.

The morning dragged by. I knew old Atwell thought I was half-asleep again, but I was really just thinking about our coach problem, and looking out the window to see if it was still raining.

"What do you see out the window all the time, Jake?" she finally asked me.

"Rain," I said.

The class laughed.

"Haven't you ever seen rain before?"

"Yes, ma'am."

"Then please pay attenion to what's happening in class."

I paid attention. We were doing a unit on explorers. De Soto, Henry Hudson, Champlain... They were all good guys and tough, too. Not knowing where they were going. Having trouble with their own men, the Indians, sickness, the weather...

The weather... I looked outside. I thought it might be raining just a wee bit harder. But was it raining on the west side of town where Vets Park was?

"Jake!"

My head snapped around. I tried to pay attention but it was hard.

Lenny was humming a little tune when I got home for lunch. Usually a good sign.

"Hello, Jake."

I barely nodded at him. It had stopped raining. It was only sprinkling. I didn't feel hungry.

"Hey, man," he said cheerfully, "couldn't you have picked out a quieter alarm clock?"

"What do you want for three dollars?" I said grumpily. His eyes opened wide. "What's the matter, kid?"

"Nothing."

I went into the kitchen and made myself a sandwich with cream cheese and poured myself a big old ugly glass of milk.

Lenny came in with a cigarette and coffee and sat down across the table from me.

"How was school?"

"Lousy."

"How come?"

"It's always lousy."

His eyes narrowed. "What'd you do bad this morning?"

"Nothing," I said.

He relaxed. "We're getting you back on the ball, so don't foul up. By the way ..." He started examining me like I was something on a shelf in a bargain store.

"Now what?"

"That thing on your back."

"What thing?"

"That shirt you're wearing. How long you been wearing it?"

"A couple of days. Why?"

"A couple of weeks looks more like it."

"It fits good."

"Yeah, but it smells bad. How many shirts do you have, Jake?"

"I got plenty."

"You got nothing. This morning I got up early and began looking through your clothes. You're wearing all your last year's stuff."

"So what?"

"It looks terrible. People will think I don't take good care of you."

"Don't worry about it. I'll tell them you do."

Lenny laughed. "I'll pick you up in the parking lot right after school's out."

"I can't, Lenny. I got a ball game."

"What time's your ball game?"

"Five thirty."

"I'll get you there by five thirty."

"I got to be at Vets Park by four."

"Four? Listen, Jake, don't feed me a line. You're not a Major Leaguer yet. Nobody eleven years old has got to be at his ball game an hour and a half early. Besides, there won't even be a ball game this afternoon because the radio just said thundershowers."

"We still got to be there even if it's raining."

"Well, you'll be there."

"But I got to be there early enough to find us a coach."

"What are you talking about, Jake?"

I finally got it through Lenny's thick skull what our problem was and how we needed an adult male to pretend for five minutes he was our coach, shake hands with the Baer Machine coach, and agree with the umps to call off the game, and then he could take off.

Old Lenny listened to me carefully, nodded, and when I was done, he said: "OK, Jake. I'll be your patsy for those five minutes. I don't have to be in Detroit till seven thirty. I can make it even if I leave by six fifteen. For this rainout, I'm your 'coach,' but first you go with me to buy some clothes."

I stuck out my hand. "You got a deal."

"And you got a coach," Lenny said.

"I'd rather have your uncle coaching us for five minutes than anyone else all season," Tony Parker said.

Ned said: "Will he hit some fly balls to us even if it's raining?"

"I'll ask him," I said.

But when I saw Lenny in the parking lot after school, I realized I could no more ask him to hit fly balls than ask the President of the United States to be a pinch hitter. Lenny was all duded up for Detroit. Pressed suit, fancy shirt and tie, and sunglasses, and calfskin shoes I'd never seen before.

I grinned. "That's no coach's uniform I even saw. I hope you ain't gonna buy me stuff like that."

Lenny smiled. "You're not worthy to be duded up like this, Jake."

"Good thing, too," I said, and we both laughed.

By the time we got through with our shopping expedition it was after five and we had to hustle to get me changed and the two of us over to Vets Park which is on the west side of town. We also had to pick up the equipment bag at the Fultons' house. I was getting nervous; Lenny tried to relax me by assuring me no one could play in a drizzle like this. The rain was coming down harder and harder though I hadn't heard any thunderclaps yet. The windshield wipers on his car were going splat-splat.

"How do I know it's raining on the west side?" I asked.

Lenny laughed. "Jake, I never thought of you as a worrier before."

"I got to worry about my team."

"Your team?"

"Yeah. I run the team."

Lenny whistled. "Isn't that taking on a lot for eleven years old?"

"I'm not eleven. I'm thirty-five."

We both laughed. It was one of those stupid things we say to each other that always made us both laugh.

We hit the west side of town, which starts west of Main Street, and it was still raining, but not as hard, I didn't think, as on our side. When we got to the parking lot at

Vets, I could see our guys huddled under a tree on the first base side of the diamond, and their bikes parked by the tree. The Baer Machine team was sitting in a couple of station wagons, making a lot of noise. That would be all they were good for. Last year we almost wiped them out in two innings, getting ten runs in the first inning. There's a rule in the ten-, eleven-, twelve-, and thirteen-year-old leagues that if you get twelve runs in two innings and the other team doesn't get any, you win right away. It's called a "wipe-out win." The Baer Machine team was the only one we'd ever come close to wiping out, but that was last year, and this year they had some new players who couldn't, I figured, be any worse than their last year's guys.

It didn't look like the umps had arrived. When I started to get out of the car, Lenny told me I was crazy. But I told him I was going to join my team. So he gave me the key to the trunk and I got out the equipment bag, hoisted it on my shoulders, tossed the keys back at him, and walked through the drizzle to the tree sheltering my guys. Ned came out to help me with the bag.

"That your uncle in the car, Jake?"

"Sure. 'Who'd you think it was?"

"I don't know. I've never seen him before. But I sure've heard about him. Will he coach us on Saturday, too?"

"He won't even coach us today. He's got more important things to do than coach a bunch of punks like us. All he does is shake hands with their coach, agree to postpone the game 'cause of rain, and take off for Detroit. Umps here yet?"

"I bet they don't even show up," Dick Williams said. We'd arrived under the tree.

"How much you want to bet?" Tony asked.

We all turned to look at the car coming into the lot. Two guys in dark blue. Umps. They got right out of their car, too, carrying their gear and a box with two new balls in it.

"They got to be kidding."

"Umps never joke."

"We ought to find an umbrella for them."

The arrival of the two umpires brought the Baer Machine clambering out of their station wagons, and their coaches and their parents. It seems every team but us has adult fans.

Only Lenny was left in his car and I knew he didn't want to get those fancy guitar-playing duds of his wet. But he got out, slowly, glaring at the sky like he was telling it to stop raining.

It didn't stop raining and Lenny put on a good sprint and arrived, all six-foot-three of him under the tree.

Everyone looked up at him. The umps, the Baer Machine team, and our guys, too. Mr. Phelps, the Baer Machine coach, came over to Lenny.

"Hello, Lenny. So they got you in the coaching business."

Lenny grinned. I could tell he didn't know who Mr. Phelps was. "Yeah," he said, "for a little while. How you been?"

"Fine. You still playing basketball?"

"No. I gave it up. I'm in the music racket now."

"So I hear. These kids of yours are good ball players, but they need a coach with a firm hand."

"I got the hands," Lenny said, with a laugh. "Don't I, Jake?"

I blushed. "Yeah."

My guys laughed.

"How's the weather look to you, Umps?" Lenny asked.

"Pretty bad, Mr. Johnson," one of the umps said. "Guess we ought to call it."

"League rules say we got to wait till five forty-five to call it, unless the diamond looks unplayable."

"That third base looks bad."

"I could put some sand on it," the other ump said. "I brought a shovel with me."

"What about home plate?"

"A little sand would help that."

"Provided it stops raining," Lenny said.

"That's right. We've got to wait another five minutes."

Lenny grinned. "I can wait five minutes."

He started chatting with the Baer Machine coach, Mr. Phelps. As I look back on it now, Lenny could have made them call the game right then and there, but he said he could wait five minutes and so we waited that five minutes. The Baer Machine kids asked us about the game with the McLeod Builders. It seemed everyone in town had heard about it. Jerry and Andy were tossing a ball back and forth. So were Tony and Danny. Lenny and Mr. Phelps were chatting and I was telling the Baer Machine first baseman how they'd robbed us of the game the other day when all of a sudden, everyone became silent.

Everyone became silent because suddenly we couldn't hear the sounds of the rain falling on the tree.

We looked up. The rain had stopped.

I looked at Lenny. He was flabbergasted. He was watching the umps taking their bases out of their equipment bag.

"You don't mean you're gonna play this game?" Lenny asked.

"Got to," an ump said.

"But look at third."

"I'll fix that in two minutes with my shovel and some sand."

Mr. Phelps clapped his hands. "OK, Baer Machine, loosen up your arms. Lenny, do you want the infield first?"

Lenny was really in a state of shock. I couldn't blame him. I had sworn to him that all he had to do was shake hands and leave for Detroit. He had to go.

He looked over at me and I nodded. "It's OK," I said. "Go."

I looked at our guys. They were looking at me wonderingly, not knowing what was going on. I felt a little sick. Now it was our turn to forfeit, and this was one they wouldn't play over.

"What do you say, Lenny?" Mr. Phelps repeated. "Do you want the infield first, or us?"

Silence. Lenny's face was grim. "We'll take it first," he said. He turned to us. "What're you guys waiting for? A silver-plate invitation? Let's go. Git"

With a gleeful shout, the Print-Ails took the field. I stayed behind trying to catch Lenny's eye, to ask him why, what about Detroit, his rehearsal. He hired that hall there by the hour. It was expensive.

"What's the matter with you, Wrather?" he snarled at me. "Didn't you hear me tell you to git?"

I got.

9.

RIGHT AWAY LENNY COULD DO SOMETHING I'D NEVER seen any other coach in our league do. He could hit spinning fouls to the catcher on purpose, slicing under the ball with his bat. He could also hit mean twisting grounders that skidded in front of you; he could hit exasperating little pop flies that drove Danny Kohl at shortstop back on the grass for diving catches, and he sent sky-high fly balls that Andy Black circled under endlessly.

In five minutes of fielding practice on a wet field, we felt like we'd never known what fielding practice was before.

The Baer Machine kids were positively bug-eyed, and so were we, and all of this from a big husky guy in a fancy suit, shirt and tie. It was too much.

Lenny called us in. "OK, guys," he said softly, "these are the facts. I didn't expect to be coaching here, but here I am. I got to be in Detroit in an hour and a half. Now I understand you got a rule in this league that any team ahead by twelve runs at the end of the second inning wins the game right then and there. Is that right?"

"Yes," we all said.

"Good." He grinned. "That's what you guys are going to do for me. You're gonna get twelve quick runs and I'm gonna get to Detroit just a couple of minutes late instead of not at all. You hear?"

We heard. We didn't quite believe, but we heard.

"Good. Now let's quick go over some basics. How do you get twelve runs fast? Put your hand down, first baseman. I'm gonna tell you. You get twelve quick runs by hitting every ball around the plate, hitting it hard, putting your head down and running. On any ball going out of the infield, I want the runner taking a big turn at second and if he thinks he's got a chance, he goes. I want everyone stealing second base."

"Even Fulton?" someone asked.

"Who's Fulton?"

John raised his hand reluctantly.

"What's the matter with you?"

"I'm slow," John said.

"You got rheumatism?"

"No. Just slow."

"Today you're fast."

"He stole two bases in our last game," I said.

That broke everyone up.

"No signals to steal," Lenny said. "Everyone goes on his own. Everyone swings at every pitch around the plate."

"Even at three and 0?" Bigler asked.

"Especially at three and 0," Lenny said. "I want home runs, first baseman, not walks or singles. I got to be in Detroit by seven thirty. This is going to be a two-inning ball game or I'm gonna stomp everyone of you into the ground."

He looked pretty fierce when he said it, and no one said a thing. Finally, Jerry Jones, grinning, asked: "What about bunts, Lenny?"

"No bunts, especially from a big strong guy like you. You hit home runs or don't bother to come back to the bench. You're the pitcher, aren't you?"

"Sometimes," Jerry said.

"Well, go and warm up and throw strikes. What's your batting order, Jake?"

"Kohl, Parker, Wrather, Black, Jones, Bigler, Fulton, Williams, Franks."

"OK, guys, I don't know your names but I know your faces and I'm holding each one of you personally responsible if I don't get to Detroit on time. Twelve runs in two innings, that's an order."

It was the craziest pep talk we'd ever got in our lives, and from the strangest-looking coach anyone had ever seen. My Uncle Lenny, six-foot-three inches and dressed to kill.

The ump called batter up. The rain had completely stopped, though it was still cloudy and dark. Third base looked peculiar, full of mud and sand. The grass was wet. I had the eerie feeling we could lose twelve to nothing just as easily as win.

Only a few fans—parents of Baer Machine—had come to watch. It wasn't a baseball kind of day. It wasn't any kind of day at all.

Danny Kohl stepped in there. Lenny cupped his hands over his mouth and called out: "Get me to Detroit on time."

It was to be one of two rallying cries during the game. I don't know what the Baer Machine team thought of it.

The pitcher came down with his first pitch and Danny stepped into it and cracked it on a line over the third baseman's head.

"Wahoo," Lenny shouted gleefully. Danny took a big turn at first and then hustled back to the bag as their left fielder showed us a good arm, rifling the ball to second on one bounce. They were a well coached team, but as I remembered from last year, they didn't have many hitters. Their pitcher had good control and a medium fast ball, but we'd hit him plenty last year, and on the basis of that one pitch to Danny, it looked like we'd hit him this year.

"Get me to Detroit on time, baby," Lenny called out.

"Twelve in two," Ned shouted at Tony, who, grinning from ear to ear, stepped in there.

Twelve in two became the other rallying cry.

Tony was first pitch swinging, too. The pitch was wide, but Tony reached across the plate and poked it into right field. Danny sped around second never hesitating and headed toward third. Foolishly their right fielder tried to get him. The kid had an arm like a girl's. He lobbed high in the air, and Tony took second on the silly throw. Two balls pitched, two men on. Even a hurry-up musician couldn't ask for more action than that. But Lenny did.

"Get me to Detroit on time, Jake," he shouted.

"Twelve in two," Ned shouted.

"I want a homer, Jake," Lenny shouted. "Nothing less

or I'll stomp you right into the ground."

I tried to ignore him and concentrate on the pitcher. Baseball was my game, not Lenny's. I didn't need him coaching me, distracting me. If he wanted to get to Detroit on time, he ought to shut up a little.

The next pitch, I had the idea, was not going to be around the plate. They would be getting the idea we were first pitching swinging, so he'd probably throw me a bad one.

I was right. The pitch came in waist high but way outside. The catcher made a good stop on it. The second pitch was low around my ankles. I don't think he wanted to throw two balls in a row, but once you let up it isn't always so easy to get in the groove again. Also the ball was wet. It wasn't raining, but the grass was wet, the infield was wet, and the air was humid.

The two and 0 pitch came in . . . high. I checked my swing.

"Three balls and no strikes," the ump called out.

Lenny shouted down at me, loud enough for the whole world to hear: "If you take this pitch, Wrather, you won't be able to sit down for a week."

I heard Andy Black, on deck behind me, start laughing. I'm sure the Baer Machine pitcher thought Lenny was kidding because he grooved the next pitch. I waited on it. That's the big thing on those slow easy pitches. Don't get anxious to kill it. Don't get out in front of it. Wait till the very last second when it's sitting there in front of you, then whip that old bat around, snap those wrists, listen to that solid sound, and watch the old white ball disappear in the mists of the outfield.

I got good wood on it and the ball took off. It went behind the left fielder and the center fielder, and the poor kid in center fell on the wet grass trying to catch up with it. That turned it into an easy home run for me.

"Step on those bags, Wrather," Lenny shouted at me. "Git your foot into those bags."

As I came around third, he said: "Git, Wrather, git."

The ball was still in the outfield, but I put on the steam and gave home plate a solid plunk with my spikes.

Andy and I slapped hands, and Jerry, and Dick, and there was the whole gang pounding me, shouting: "Twelve in two. Twelve in two."

Bigler nudged me. "Look who just arrived."

I followed his look over to the wooden stands behind first. There was Mr. Fredericks, the league president, sitting alone.

"How long's he been here?"

"Just got here. I bet he came to check on us."

"Let him check."

Mr. Fredericks was looking at Lenny as though he'd never seen a baseball coach in a fancy suit, shirt, and tie and wearing sunglasses on a cloudy dark afternoon. I had to laugh. Now Mr. Fredericks would probably make a rule about what the well-dressed coach is supposed to wear.

"C'mon, number four," Lenny called down, "be a hitter up there."

Old Andy wanted to do right by Lenny so he swung

at the first pitch which was over his head and missed it by a mile.

"I never knew a number-four hitter who could hit bad pitches yet," Lenny called out. It was his way of calming Andy down.

Andy dug in. Big shouldered, narrow-waisted, he was going to be a great fullback some day. He could muscle a baseball better than anyone I knew.

The Baer Machine pitcher cleverly threw him another bad ball, hoping old Andy would go fishing again. Andy did.

"Strike two!"

"How about waiting for one in the strike zone, big guy?" Lenny called out. One big jock getting on another one.

Andy was rattled up there. I could tell; even though his broad face revealed nothing. I could see him deciding not to swing at the next one. He didn't.

It was in there.

"You're out," the ump said.

Andy walked back to the bench without looking at anyone. He sat down beside me and buried his face in his hands.

"Hey, man, cut it out. Everyone strikes out now and then."

"Yeah, but we got to get your uncle to Detroit on time."

"Nuts to him. We're playing baseball. You got to stop listening to him. Play your game, hit your pitches. Forget about him." I clapped him on the shoulder. "You'll get another crack at that pitcher."

What I didn't realize was how soon Andy would get another crack. Here we were, in the first inning, 3-0, one out, and Jerry was up. From that moment on, mayhem broke loose.

Jerry sent a high fly into center field. The centerfielder started forward, then had to reverse himself and get back. He slipped again on the grass, and the ball fell behind him. Jerry ended up on third. He wasn't there long when John Fulton slapped a sizzling ground ball that bounced off the pitcher's knees. Jerry scored and John got to first safely. Bigler laid down his usual bunt and got on. Then Dick Williams who was a streak hitter but usually started his streaks the end of July just before the season ended, hit a fly ball down the line in right field. John scored, and so did Bigler who almost overtook John coming into home. Baer Machine changed pitchers, bringing in their first baseman to pitch, but it didn't do them any good. Danny Kohl got his second hit of the inning, an infield single to deep short. Tony Parker chopped down on a pitch and by the time the pitcher caught it, he was on and Danny was on second. I was up for the second time. I took one pitch for a strike, just to see what this new pitcher looked like. Then when he threw the pitch in the same place again, I laced it into right center for an easy double. Two more runs scored. Six runs batted in in one inning for me. It was a little scary. I didn't dare look at Lenny. I mean, all these years I'd been telling him how good I am, and in the first inning I knock in six runs. It's enough to make a guy real humble.

But if Lenny was satisfied, he didn't show it. He kept shouting: "Get me to Detroit on time, fellas. Twelve in two. Twelve in two."

We already had nine, and three more didn't seem too hard. Baer Machine was falling apart right in front of us. No chatter, no hustle, they kept looking up at the sky.

It was getting darker, and once in a while you could feel tiny drops of rain. Now we were rooting for it not to rain.

They decided to change pitchers again, bringing in their catcher. All this used-up time because the catcher had to take off his equipment. He took his shin guards off very, very slowly.

"They're stalling, Ump," Bigler shouted, reminding me of Mr. McLeod in the last game.

The ump smiled. He knew what we wanted, but there wasn't any way to make their catcher go faster.

The drops fell a little faster. But it still wasn't bad. We could play. Finally their catcher had his equipment off and he went out to the mound to warm up.

"He only gets six pitches," Bigler shouted.

"Shut up, Bigler," I said.

We waited while their catcher warmed up. He couldn't throw any better than the other two guys, but he took a lot longer between warm-ups. And meanwhile, their first baseman was having a hard time making the shin guards fit. John Fulton offered his help, but the kid declined it.

"Batter up," Bigler shouted.

They finally got all set, and Andy Black stepped in. I took a big lead off second.

"Give it a ride, Andy," I shouted.

Andy obliged. He belted the ball way over the left fielder's head for a two-run homer. I waited at the plate to congratulate him. As he came around third, Lenny stepped over and swatted him on the behind. "I always knew you were my number-four hitter, man."

Andy had a big grin as he came across home plate.

Eleven runs in the first inning. One more, and then all we had to do was strike out as fast as we could, and then strike them out as fast as we could, and the game would be over.

Jerry was up next. Trying to duplicate Andy's feat he popped up. Never try to hit a home run. They just come when you're swinging in a groove. Two out. John Fulton was up next. He hit a grounder right at the third baseman who backed up, grabbed it, and threw John out.

We'd finished our licks one run short. All we had to do now was hold them, get one more run in the top of the second, and wipe them out in their bottom half.

Lenny stopped Jerry on his way to the mound. "No fooling around out there, Pitch. Just chuck that old fast one in there and mow those boys down. You hear?"

"I hear, man," Jerry said.

It was raining a little harder, but still OK. I got a knot in my stomach just thinking about it.

Jerry took two pitches and Lenny called out: "My man's all warmed up. Let's move this old ball game along."

"Batter up," the ump said promptly. He didn't like getting wet either.

But their batter took his own sweet time moving into the box. First he had a conference with his coach. We all shouted "stalling" but it didn't hurry them.

Finally though he got in there. Jerry was so anxious to strike him out that he poured his fast ball in there about five feet high. John just let it go.

Jerry's second pitch was a shovel ball and John scooped it out of the mud.

"Time," Lenny said, and he trotted out to the mound in his fancy white suit, avoiding the wet spots, making Jerry come off the muddy mound to talk with him on the grass.

"What're you trying to do, Pitch? Make me late for my rehearsal?"

Jerry giggled. I was annoyed. This was no time for a comedy act. I kicked the dirt.

Lenny kicked his leg in the air. "Get your left leg out there. I know it's slippery, but make a hole right there .. . no back there. OK . . . now that's where your left foot should go. Then you swing around with your pitch and follow through. You got a whole body on you to help that big arm of yours. You get as much control from your hips as from your arm. Now try it."

Right then and there, he gave Jerry a pitching lesson. I didn't even know Lenny knew anything about pitching. He'd played first in high school and in semipro ball.

Jerry went through the motions. "I got it."

"OK. Now no fancy stuff. Just get that left leg out,

and follow it with your body and throw that ball into the catcher's glove. They'll never see it."

Lenny went back to the bench. It was an amazing performance. Nobody had ever told Jerry anything about pitching before. We all assumed he was so good because he was natural. But I learned you can make the natural more effective with good coaching.

Jerry got his left foot way out there, followed it around, and the pitch smoked across the plate for a strike. "Now you got it," Lenny called out.

That did it for Baer Machine right then and there. Jerry's left foot came out and the Bear Machine batters went down one, two, three. They never even saw the ball.

"Hustle in, boys," Lenny called out.

The rain was coming down a little harder now. Only a few fans were left, and they were under umbrellas. Most of the others had gone to their cars and were watching from the parking lot.

Mr. Phelps, the Baer Machine coach had gone over to the stands and was talking with Mr. Fredericks. I had a good idea what they were talking about. When to call a game.

"Let's go, guys," I shouted. "Let's get a batter in there. Bigler, get in there. Forget about the doughnut. Get in there and bunt the ball."

"Batter up," Ned shouted.

But the Baer Machine pitcher went on taking his warm-up pitches.

Mr. Phelps came back from his conference. "Lenny,

don't you think it's getting a little wet to play ball?"

"Depends on who's winning," Lenny said, with a grin. "Me, I've never been drier in my life. Let's keep going."

Mr. Phelps hesitated, shrugged, and nodded to the umps. For the first time this season I was glad we had a male coach. If Mrs. Fulton were here, we'd have been walking home by now.

Bigler stepped in. The pitcher took his time, wiped his face. The drizzle was harder now.

"Step into it, First Baseman," Lenny called out. "All we need is a little old homer."

Lenny didn't know that all Jeff did was bunt. But Jeff, listening to Lenny, knew he had to swing on the first pitch. He swung on a bad ball and popped it up. Their third baseman grabbed it.

That brought up Dick Williams. Dick had got a lucky hit in the first inning, down the right field line. I could see him thinking he could do it again. He swung on the first pitch, too, and popped it up to the first baseman.

"C'mon, guys," I shouted, "forget about the rain. Wait on your pitches. You hear? Wait on your pitches."

"Hit it out of here, Ned."

"No pitcher in there, Neddy."

I looked at Ned up there and my heart sank. Our last chance to win this game in two innings. Ned was strong but fat. He'd have to hit that ball three miles to hit a home run. Still, if he got a double, then Danny ...

The first pitch was way high, and Ned let it go by.

"That's the eye, Ned."

"We got to swing, Jake," Tony said.

"Not at bad pitches. Never at bad pitches."

The next pitch was in there and Ned really walloped it. It went into left field on the line. The left fielder charged it, trying to make a shoestring catch. He didn't. The ball skidded in front of him and went right through his legs. And there was fat old Ned legging and puffing and chugging away, and all of us up and screaming at him. The left fielder had reached the ball. He had that good arm. Lenny was coaching at third. Ned was around second and coming toward third. It was up to Lenny. Ned would never make it home against a good throw. Lenny was the one who needed this twelfth run so badly. Ned was too slow to leg it home safely. It was up to Lenny to hold him. Hold him, Lenny, I prayed. Play baseball.

Lenny held up his hands. "Hold it," he shouted.

But either Ned couldn't or wouldn't hear him. With the rain coming down, everyone screaming, third base a slippery shifting sea of mud, that fat old jackass Ned Franks hit the inside of the bag, made a wide turn and kept going for home. He couldn't have stopped even if he wanted to.

"Oh, no," we groaned.

"That's it."

We watched and waited. The left fielder threw. A beautiful throw, low and accurate right on the plate. Ned would be out by ten feet. The only thing he could do was crash into the catcher and make him drop the ball. It was a substitute catcher.

"Hit him, Ned," I shouted.

"Hit him."

Ned hit him. He rumbled into him like a big old express train, and the kid and Ned tumbled together into the mud.

"Out," the ump shouted. "No, safe!"

The ball trickled out of their embrace and rolled to a resting stop in the mud.

Safe!

We'd made it.

Twelve to zip. We ran screaming to Ned and began pounding him, kissing him, hugging him, trying to hoist him onto our shoulders, collapsing under his weight, and while we were doing this, the rain came down.

The rain came down from the skies.

It emptied out of the skies.

The fattest rain you ever saw, great globs of it, pouring, pelting, turning the field into a quagmire, making everyone run for trees, cars, umbrellas. Our guys didn't run though, they just kept jumping up and down screaming hysterically: "Twelve in two, twelve in two—we made it!"

But they were wrong. It wasn't twelve in two at all. It was twelve in one and one half innings. We had to give Baer Machine their bats, and no one could bat in this rain, no one could play on this diamond for another twenty-four hours.

The thunder started then, and lightning. I wanted to cry. If there wasn't so much water around already, I would have cried.

I stood with Lenny under the tree. And the guys stood there, too, and slowly it dawned on them, from our two faces, that something was wrong, and so I told them what was wrong. As the umpires pulled the bases stakes out and ran for their car, I told the Print-Alls we'd just wasted twelve runs and that the game would have to be played over again.

It was like air going out of a balloon... No one said a thing. We were getting soaked, but no one moved.

Mr. Phelps, wet to his skin, came over to us. "That's tough luck, boys. I'm sorry."

I think he meant it, too. He turned to Lenny. "I don't know what your coaching tricks are, Lenny, but you sure fired your team up. Do you want me to call you to arrange the make-up game or do you want to call me?"

He thought Lenny was our real coach. Lenny stood there, his face wet, his white suit soaked through, his purple shirt and yellow tie a mess. . . .

"We'll arrange it, Coach," he said. "I'll have one of the boys get in touch with you."

They shook hands.

Although the rain was pouring through the shelter of our tree, Lenny didn't move. We didn't either. He turned to Ned. "Didn't you hear me tell you to wait up?"

Ned shook his head, "I remember you said: Keep running. Go on your own."

Lenny had to smile. "You were on your own all right. Out by ten feet." He slapped Ned on the back. "Good going."

He turned to us.

"I know it's wet, but I want to say something to you boys. You made me real proud." His voice was soft, he kept wiping his face with a handkerchief. "You hit, you hustled, you played like a bunch of major leaguers. You did everything I asked you to. You got the twelve runs and I'm gonna get to Detroit on time—a little wet, but on time." He smiled crookedly. "You didn't win it, and I know that hurts. But for me," he leaned forward, "you're one bunch of gutsy winners."

He looked at me. "Jake, how you gonna get home?"

"I'll ride with Andy on his bike."

"Say, Mr. Johnson," Danny Kohl said.

"Lenny's my name, Mister Shortstop."

"Lenny… will you coach us again?"

Lenny smiled. Like he knew it was coming and what was he going to do? Duck, get hit by the pitch, or hit it. He hit it. Honestly but sadly.

"Can't do it, Mister Shortstop. Much as I'd like to because you boys are one sweet team. But I got to make my music rehearsals in Detroit, and that's the size of it. Jake, you and Andy hustle the equipment to the car. I'll open the trunk for you. See you guys. You were beautiful."

With that Lenny took off into the rain with those long basketball strides of his. Andy and I walked slowly, sharing the load of the equipment bag. Lenny threw the key out the window to me. I caught it, put the bag in, locked the trunk, and gave him the key back.

"Change into dry clothes when you get home, Jake,

and heat up some pea soup. And get to bed early."

I nodded. Just before he closed his car window I said something I don't usually say to that big galoot of an uncle of mine: "Thanks."

He winked at me, and took off in a squeal of tires. We stood in the rain and watched him go. The others came around.

"Boy, he's something else," Jerry said.

"You got a great uncle," Bigler said.

"I wish I had an uncle like that," Tony said.

"Jake, you're lucky, you know that."

I couldn't believe my ears. There we were, standing in the rain having had another victory taken away from us—the second in a row—and they were telling me how lucky I was to be living with Lenny and then how great it would be if we could find a place in Arborville where Lenny and his rock band could rehearse and maybe then he could stay and coach us … and on and on they went, wet to the skin, water running down their faces, looking like they were standing at the bottom of the ocean. And happy. Crazy happy.

"You guys are nuts," I said. "Let's go home."

It was a long wet bicycle ride home, but it didn't stop them from making all kinds of stupid plans about finding a place for Lenny's band in Arborville. After a while I got so wet I didn't hear a thing and didn't care either.

10.

Smoke rings went back and forth between the cowboy and the cowgirl like they were trying to lasso each other. But the banging wasn't coming from them. It was coming from somewhere else—like the front door!

I opened my eyes all the way. I got up, turned off the TV, and went to the door. There was Jeff Bigler and Danny Kohl grinning at me in the middle of the night.

"Jake, when you sleep you sleep," Bigler said.

I blinked at them. "How do you know I been sleeping?" "We've been watching you through the window." "Do you always watch TV when you sleep?"

"Haha. What do you guys want? What time is it?"

"Ten thirty. Listen, Jake, we're onto something big."

"Put your shoes on and come with us."

"Are you two guys nuts?"

"Nope," Bigler said. "Danny and I found a way for your Uncle Lenny to coach us regularly."

"You're nuts, both of you. There isn't no way at all for him to coach us."

"Get your sneaks on and follow us."

"Where to?"

"West Hoover Street."

"What's there?"

"An empty music studio."

"You guys taking dope or something?"

Danny laughed. "Don't argue for once, Jake. Come on."

I wouldn't follow Bigler around the block, but Danny Kohl's a pretty level-headed kid, so maybe something really was up. I got into my sneaks and we headed down Packard Road. Packard is a big street with lots of cars and I knew the first police car that came along would stop us. There's a curfew in this town for kids under sixteen, and I think it's ten o'clock on weekdays. Danny and Jeff told me they'd sneaked out their backdoors. I guess I was the only guy on the Print-Alls could walk out his front door any time of day or night.

We got off Packard as soon as we could and cut through side streets till we hit East Hoover. We walked west on it till we crossed Main Street. The place we were going to, they said, was just one block west of Main and we were standing in front of it before I knew we were there.

"That's it," Danny said.

"What's it?"

"Your uncle's new studio, so he doesn't have to go to Detroit to rehearse," Bigler said.

"You guys should be locked up."

All I saw was a long low building, no lights on inside, nothing but dark walls. It looked like a small prison if it looked like anything. And what it was doing smack in the middle of a residential neighborhood I didn't know.

"Come on, Jeff. Let's show him around."

The two of them walked up to the building like they

owned it, but then the act was over. They didn't go in the front door for the good reason that the front door was locked. They went around the side to an open window and climbed in.

"You guys can get arrested for this," I said.

"Shhh," Bigler said. "Come on up."

"You're crazy."

"Jake, are you scared?"

Was I scared? No, I wasn't scared. I'm not scared of anything except them trying to break up me and Lenny, but what's the sense in busting into a building in the middle of the night for no good reason?

Danny stuck his head out the window. "Come on, Jake, before people see you."

I jumped up and boosted myself over the windowsill and dropped down onto a cement floor. I crouched down inside and looked around. At first I couldn't see a thing; all I smelled was dampness and felt some cobwebs.

"What is this place?"

"Shhh," Bigler said. "I'll find the light switch."

"Don't turn on the lights, you nut," Danny said.

While they argued, I began to make out things inside the building: crates, buckets, piles of lumber, sacks of things. It was obviously a warehouse. But with lots of empty space in it.

Danny lit a match and we looked around. Boxes and boxes all over, but the place was big.

"What's in those boxes?"

"Bring the match over here, Danny."

"Ouch."

"Light another one."

"Why don't you light one?"

"I don't have any matches."

"Shhh, both of you. Danny, light a match. Good. Bring it here."

"What's it say, Jake?"

"Asphalt shingles."

"This says nails."

"Some lumber."

"Heck," Danny said, "it's just an old warehouse. We can clean it up for Lenny."

"Nothing doing."

"Jake, do you want to forfeit the rest of the schedule?"

"No, but this is crazy."

"What do we got to lose?" Bigler asked. "We can clean this up tomorrow and you get your uncle and bring him over here around four thirty and see if he likes it. Then he can rehearse with his band here. He won't have to go to Detroit anymore and he can coach the team. It's perfect."

"Perfectly nuts. Someone owns this place."

"If Lenny likes it, we go to the guy and get his permission."

"Just like that."

"Sure. The important thing is that we get a coach by Saturday for the make-up game against the McLeod Builders. You got to admit that's the important thing."

I had to admit it was. We climbed out the window and went home. It was close to midnight when I got back to our house. As I walked onto the porch I saw the venetian blinds in the Witherspoon front window rattle and there was old Mrs. Witherspoon giving me the evil eye.

I waved to her. What else should I do? And went inside and to bed. I didn't fall asleep right away. Part of it was the nap I'd already had on the couch and part was sheer excitement about the old warehouse. It was a crazy scheme but just crazy enough to work. We'd have to clean it up real good. Lenny would have to like it for music; we'd have to find out who owned it and how you did that I didn't know. Go to City Hall, ask people in the neighborhood. It was too much. I fell asleep thinking maybe the Print-Alls would end up as a bunch of detectives rather than ball players.

Darminumming! The old firebell went off at seven thirty and just to show you how used to things a guy gets, old Lenny didn't stir a bit. Which meant he got in late. His clothes were lying all over. I skipped milk and made myself some coffee and grabbed a chunk of cheese, put it on some bread. After breakfast, I left a note. Ordinarily I don't leave notes for Lenny, but just in case he was thinking of not being around at noon, I wrote:

"I got to talk to you at noon—Jake."

A big old hairy soccer game was going on in front of Sampson School. Neither Bigler nor Danny Kohl were around so I got into the game. There's an art to entering soccer games. If you wait for someone to ask you in, or holler "joiners" you might as well forget it. The idea is to slip in with another kid, and if there is no other kid who wants to get in, just sort of amble onto the field, pick a side, and pretend you've been there since the beginning.

Tony Parker and John Fulton were on one side so I decided to get on their team. The ball was bouncing around with a dozen feet kicking at it.

"Wait a second," I shouted.

Play stopped. Everyone looked at me.

"The way you guys are kicking, someone's going to get hurt." While I was making my speech, I saw John Fulton move off to the right. He read me pretty well.

"Give me the ball," I growled.

Someone kicked the ball over to me.

"Only one person kicks at a time," I said, and kicked the ball over to John. "Let's get a goal, John," I shouted, and we were off running.

Was that other team mad! They chased us, shouting "cheat," "unfair," "you called time," but John passed it to Tony who could really keep the ball around the toe of his sneaker. He had a shot at the goal but he faked it, drawing the goalie to him and he passed it sideways over to me. I laid into it, and the ball went flying between the posts for a score.

"Jake, you cheated."

"It doesn't count."

"Start it over."

"Jake called time."

But the game went on. It went on because it didn't really make any difference who won or lost. Everyone changed sides the next day anyway. It was the opposite of baseball where you became a team and stayed a team. Which is why you fought to stay together when they tried to break you up.

The bell rang, breaking up the game. Tony, John, and I walked toward the school. They had heard about the warehouse and wanted to know what my uncle would think about it.

"I bet he'll think we're nuts. Don't count on a thing."

"Well," Tony said grimly, "we got to count on it. It's our only chance to play a ball game Saturday against the McLeod Builders."

If that was our only chance, I thought, then God help us.

A long morning in school, and during most of it, when I could stay awake, I thought about the silly warehouse and how Lenny had to see it and how the guys were going to clean it up this afternoon.

Twice old Atwell called on me for answers I didn't have. I didn't even hear the questions.

Finally she asked me what time I'd gone to bed last night.

I told her eight thirty, which was when I fell asleep on the couch. She looked disbelieving, but that was her problem.

At noon, I met Bigler, Ned, and Danny and the other guys.

"Four thirty," Jeff reminded me. "Bring your uncle

down then. Not before then or we won't have time to get it cleaned up."

"Have you found out yet who owns it?"

"That'll come later."

"Suppose the guy doesn't give us permission and we've cleaned it up?"

"Tough for us. But we got to play this one inning at a time. If we clean it up and Jake's uncle likes it, then we'll get permission."

Old Bigler was talking tough. I hoped he knew what he was doing.

"OK," I said, "I'll get him down at four thirty. But does he have to climb in the bloody window?"

Dick Williams laughed.

So did Ned. "I bet your uncle's climbed in lots of windows."

"Yeah," Jerry said, "but not now. Not in those duds he wears now."

"We'll have the front door open for him," Bigler said, "and a red carpet out."

"Suppose someone calls the cops," Ned said.

"We'll roll the carpet in," Dick Williams laughed.

"No one will call the cops," Jeff said. "Let's get our signals straight. Jake brings his uncle at four thirty. The rest of us meet there right after school. Every guy brings a broom, a mop, and a bucket. Right?"

Everyone agreed. The plan was in operation.

To my surprise, Lenny was up, drinking coffee in the kitchen, and he had an ominous mean look about him, like he was waiting for me to get home.

"Get my note?" I asked cheerfully.

"Sit down, Jake," he said abruptly.

"Sure, what's the matter?"

"I got called from school again."

"You did?"

"Yeah. And I had an interesting conversation with old lady Witherspoon next door."

I began to see the connection.

"Miss Bradsbury said you were half-asleep in school this morning, and Mrs. Witherspoon said she saw you come in at midnight. OK, Jake, what's going on? You told me you were going to bed early."

"I did, but I woke up and went for a walk."

He thought I was kidding him. A long basketball hand reached out and snatched me up tight.

"Jake," Lenny said softly, "I got no time for this kind of stuff. Old Raspberry wants to see me at four. I got our studio in Detroit reserved from five o'clock on. It costs us fifty bucks a crack for that hall in Detroit, Jake. I'm throwing away fifty bucks because of a kid named Jake Wrather who happens to be my nephew, and I want to know now what this kid Jake Wrather is doing walking the streets of Arborville at midnight."

"Let me go."

"Talk first."

"I ain't ever gonna talk with you squeezing me."

He let me go.

"OK," I said, stepping back. "Bigler and Danny Kohl

came over and we went for a walk. That's all. You can ask them."

"You went for a walk. Till midnight?"

"That's right. They wanted to show me a building … over on West Hoover. They want to use it as a … clubhouse."

"Jake, you're lying to me."

"Honest, Lenny, I'm not. I'll show the place to you this afternoon."

"We're going to see old Raspberry this afternoon."

"After Raspberry."

"After Raspberry I'm going to beat your butt and then go to Detroit."

"You can beat my butt, then let me show you this place. we walked to."

"Jake," Lenny said softly, "what am I going to do with you?"

"Trust me," I said.

"What are we going to do about you two?" Old Raspberry looked from Lenny to me and back again. She didn't sound mad. Worse, she sounded tired.

"Mrs. Atwell is at the end of her rope with Jake. We've had social worker reports for over a year stating what a very unusual situation it is to have an eleven-year-old boy being brought up by his twenty-four-year-old uncle who works nights in Detroit. Lenny, I've had complaints from parents who say that Jake is a bad influence on their sons. He stays out all hours of the night, he has no rules. I used to have an answer for these parents. I used to be able to say: I believe Jake's going to be all right. He's tough, but he's had to be tough. But he's smart, too. He's got potential. He's a leader. But I'm not so sure anymore. This morning Jake fell asleep in class. So did Jeff Bigler and Danny Kohl. I've learned they were both out with you last night, Jake."

I opened my mouth to protest. To tell her it was they who had woken me up, and made me go out. But one thing would lead to another and I knew this was not the moment to reveal our plan about the warehouse. It would only get Lenny in deeper trouble with old Raspberry.

"Is that right, Jake? Were the three of you out together last night?"

"Yes, ma'am."

She was silent. Lenny sat there without saying a word. It was funny, his being here, too, because I was sure she used to send for him years ago. He was in one of the pictures hanging on the wall.

"Lenny," old Raspberry said, "unless there is an immediate change in Jake's behavior, I am going to recommend that steps be taken to place him in a foster home."

Lenny shrugged. "He's getting to be a big kid. He could be trouble for a foster home."

"But he's no trouble for you?"

"He's trouble for me," Lenny admitted. "It's not easy on either of us. I think I can straighten him out though."

"How?"

"Talking to him."

"I don't think that will work, Lenny. I think he needs

you home more than you have been home."

I was dying to tell them both about our plan, but I couldn't. It could only wreck it.

Lenny was silent.

"Unless you find a way to stay home nights, Lenny, I'm afraid that a foster home is definitely in the cards for Jake."

Lenny stood up.

"I'd like to talk this over with Jake."

"I hope you will. I'm sorry to have made you come in like this."

"It's OK," Lenny said. "Nice seeing you again."

He smiled when he said it, and she smiled, too. And I could see Lenny as a little kid there, just like me.

He wasn't smiling though when we got out to the car.

"OK, Jake, we have our talk now."

"Let's go to our clubhouse and talk."

"Don't clubhouse me, we talk here and now."

"Lenny, I told you I got a place for us to talk. I swear I'll do anything you say if you just come down there with me."

He sighed. "You always got to have your way, don't you?"

I got in the car. "You won't regret it."

He smiled. "Jake, you're too much. Sometimes I wonder if I'm not really hurting you, bringing you up like this. Maybe I ought to ship you to West Virginia."

"Hey, cut that talk out. You're making me nervous."

"I don't know," he said. "I just don't know."

When Lenny sounded like that—tired and beaten, I really got scared. I guess there's a point in every man's life when it's just as easy to quit as to fight and win. I hope I never reach that point with anything, but I suddenly had the scared feeling sitting in the car in the school parking lot that Lenny was right there. He was ready to quit on us as a team.

"Start the car," I commanded. "I'll tell you how to get there."

11.

I N T H E D A Y T I M E T H E S C A R Y W A R E H O U S E W A S J U S T A P L A I N
old cement block building. And from the outside there
was no way of telling that the Print-Alls were inside cleaning it up. In fact, the absence of any signs of life made me
wonder if something had gone wrong.

But it was too late to change my mind; our course was
committed.

"If that's your clubhouse," Lenny said, "that old thing's
been here as long as I can remember."

"You ever been inside?"

"No."

"Come in then. It's a good place to talk."

"No place is a good place to talk about what we got to
talk about, Jake."

"What's that?" I was hardly listening to him, worrying
whether there had been a hitch in the plans and the guys
had got chased out of there.

"About us splitting, which is what is going to happen unless I can figure out a way to spend more time in
Arborville."

We were at the front door. I made a little prayer that
the front door would be unlocked, that the guys were
inside, that the place would be cleaned up, that Lenny

would like it, that he could stay nights in Arborville, that we wouldn't split up, that he'd coach our team regularly.

Come to think of it, it wasn't such a little prayer after all.

I gave a dum-de-de-dum-dum-de-dum knock on the door as though it were a signal. The door opened right away, and there was Dick Williams standing there, his face dirty but creased by a grin.

"Hello, Jake. Hello, Lenny."

"Hello, Centerfielder," Lenny said. "What're you doing here?"

"Welcoming you," Dick said, and stepped to one side. Lenny and I went in. I took a couple of steps inside, and then the realization of what they'd done hit me. I stood there gaping. The place was beautiful. Swept up, mopped, all boxes stacked neatly along one wall, and the whole warehouse had been turned into a large clean room. And down from the ceiling, on two pieces of string hung a big old wobbly sign that said in big crayon letters:

THIS IS LENNY JOHNSON'S MUSIC STUDIO
REHEARSALS & RECORDINGS
QUIET, PLEASE!

I looked up at Lenny. For the first time I saw that old sweat stuck for words. He was staring at the sign, and then at the whole place. Dick Williams put two fingers inside his mouth and blew.

The whistle brought action. Out from behind boxes popped the rest of the guys, dirty but grinning.

Lenny looked at them and let out a soft whistle. "Man, oh, man, what is going on here?"

Bigler came up to us. "Lenny, we got a trade to make with you. You coach us and we let you use this place to rehearse your band."

Lenny looked at Jeff as though Jeff had stepped off another planet.

"You are gonna let me use this place?"

"What's wrong with it?"

"Nothing's wrong with it, man. It's beautiful." Lenny walked around the room. "It's big and beautiful and made to keep sound inside."

"It's got electricity, too," Jeff said.

"And running water," Danny Kohl said. He turned on a tap in a wall sink.

"There's a toilet," Ned Franks said.

"That works," Tony added.

"'Cause I used it," old Andy said, and looked embarrassed right after he said it.

We laughed, but our eyes followed Lenny anxiously as he walked around the room examining it, the stuff in it. He stopped before a clipboard hanging on the wall. I didn't like the way he was looking at it.

"Well, is it a trade?" I asked.

No answer.

"Hey, you got plenty of room for drums," Bigler called

out hopefully.

"It's as good as any place in Detroit," Danny said.

"And there's room to park out back," Bigler added.

"Don't you hear us, Lenny?" I said. "You don't have to go to Detroit anymore."

"No more driving," Bigler said.

"You can stay in town and coach us," I said.

When there was still no sound from his mouth, no motion from his back, I got exasperated and yelled: "Say something!"

Lenny turned around, the clipboard in his hands. There was a faint grin on his lips.

"I'll say you kids got a lot of nerve, that's what I'll say." It wasn't at all what we'd expected him to say.

"Do you have any idea who owns this building?"

A sick feeling hit my stomach. We avoided each other's eyes.

"Who?" Danny Kohl, braver than the rest of us, asked.

"The McLeod Building Company. Mr. Pat McLeod, president. This is their main warehouse on the west side of town."

No one said a thing. What was there to say? The building of our enemy—the team and the coach that hated us the most, that wanted us broken up.

Ned Franks turned to Jeff Bigler. "You big dope."

"How was I supposed to know?"

"You could have found out."

Dick Williams slumped down on a pile of lumber. "All that work for nothing."

"Bigler, I'm going to strangle you," Tony said.

Jeff looked away. "It seemed like a good idea." "You could have found out."

"All that work … for nothing," Dick repeated.

Jerry Jones looked around the room. "You know what I'm gonna do? I'm gonna muss this place over."

He was going to kick over a sack of nails.

"Hold on," I said. "What've we got to lose by talking to Mr. McLeod?"

"You're kidding, Jake. He hates us."

"OK, so he hates us. He's a businessman, ain't he? Maybe he would rent this place to Lenny. What do you pay in Detroit for that hall?"

Lenny had been watching us with interest. Like he was trying to see what our reaction to disaster would be.

"Two hundred a week."

"Suppose you offer half of that to Mr. McLeod? He's not making anything off this place now. What's he got to lose? What've we got to lose?"

"Jake's right," Jerry said.

"Who's gonna deal with him?"

"Jake."

"He hates Jake."

"That's OK," I said. "He can hate me all he wants. It's a business proposition. I'll talk to him at the game tomorrow morning."

"What game?"

"The make-up game. Tomorrow's Saturday in case you guys have forgot."

"Who's gonna coach us?"

I turned to Lenny. "You don't rehearse tomorrow morning, how about coaching us one more time?"

Lenny smiled. "Are you punks asking me to get up in the morning to watch you play your version of baseball?"

"Yeah," I growled, "that's just what we're asking you to do. We cleaned this place up for you."

Lenny laughed. "OK. I'll coach you tomorrow morning."

"I got an idea," Ned Franks said. "We can throw the game to Mr. McLeod and put him in a good humor and then, Jake, you'll ask him."

"Nothing doing. We're gonna beat the pants off those guys, even if it is our last game. Our proposition is strictly business. Right?"

They didn't answer me. They were all looking at the front door. I looked, too. Standing in the doorway were two men: one I didn't recognize at first because he was out of uniform, the other I knew only because he was in uniform.

The first man was McLeod himself; the second man was a tense Arborville policeman.

Mr. McLeod said: "What's going on here?"

The policeman said: "Hello, Lenny," and relaxed.

For the first time in my life I was relieved as well as proud that everyone in Arborville knew my uncle. But, though the policeman had relaxed, Mr. McLeod hadn't.

"What are you boys doing here? Don't you know that this is private property?"

"How're you doing, Nick?" Lenny asked the cop. "Fine, big Lenny. You still playing ball?"

"Nah. Gave it up. You?"

"I'm playing for Sims Stores in the Municipal league in the winter." The policeman turned to Mr. McLeod who was flabbergasted by this exchange. "I used to play on the same high school team with Lenny Johnson, Mr. McLeod. Lenny, this is Mr. McLeod who owns this building. We got a complaint from neighbors that kids had gone in through a window."

"We only went in through the window because the front door was locked," Jeff Bigler said.

"Whether you went in the window or the front door," Mr. McLeod said angrily, and I figured he was twice as mad because the policeman and Lenny were old friends, "you're still trespassing on private property."

"Yeah," Bigler said, "but we didn't know it was your property."

"Shut up, Bigler," I said.

At those two words, Mr. McLeod's expression changed. It hadn't dawned on me that he didn't know who we were —that we, out of uniform—were just as unfamiliar as he out of uniform. But at that old refrain of "Shut up, Bigler," he suddenly recognized us.

"Why it's the Print-All team," he said. "And by the looks of it, every single one of you. All right, you can start explaining now."

Everyone looked at me to start talking, and so I did. I explained why we had come in early to clean this place up, what our hopes were…

While I talked, Mr. McLeod began to realize for the first time that his messy old warehouse was spotlessly clean, that everything was neatly stacked, and for the first time he was aware of the sign hanging down from the middle that told the whole world this was Lenny Johnson's Music Studio.

The cop and Lenny didn't say a word. They just stood there watching Mr. McLeod.

I went on and explained how the only available man coach was my uncle and how he had to go to Detroit to rehearse, but how we thought this old warehouse could serve as a studio for him and he could stay in town long enough to coach us. I didn't say anything about this warehouse keeping Lenny and me together as a family because that was none of his business. No one knew about that but me and Lenny. Finally, I told Mr. McLeod it would strictly be a business proposition. I mean, Lenny would pay.

It didn't come out as smoothly as it sounds. I mean, I hummed and hawed but no one said a thing till I was done and Lenny didn't interrupt me to help me out once. Which is why I like living with him—he puts me on my own.

I could tell his policeman friend liked what I said. He was nodding. Lenny didn't give a thing away but I knew he thought this place could work as a studio for his band. It all depended on Mr. McLeod—on how big he was willing to let himself be.

It turned out to be not very much.

"I never heard of such a crazy story in my life," he snapped. "This is a warehouse for building materials, not a sound studio."

"It could be both," Bigler said, quickly. "A warehouse in the daytime and a sound studio at night. We'd clean it up for both you guys for nothing."

"What about the noise, Lenny?" the policeman asked.

"The cement blocks would keep most of it in," Lenny said. "Probably all."

"Sounds like a good idea to me," the policeman said. "What do you think, Mr. Mac?"

"I'm wondering what kind of law and order we're going to have in this town if you think a bunch of kids breaking into a building is a good idea."

"Now hold on," the cop said, getting red in the face. If there's anything a policeman doesn't like it's getting chewed out in public, especially in front of a bunch of kids—"these kids broke in all right and I don't condone that, but they meant well. Heck, they've been cleaning the place up."

"For their own selfish reasons. I want all of you out and right now. If I wanted a bunch of kids in this warehouse I'd tell you. I don't like the way this team plays ball; I don't like the way they take over other people's property. And if I were you, Mr. Johnson, I'd put a close watch on your nephew Jake. He almost gave one of my players a concussion by tagging him in the head."

And on and on he went…

And so that was it. Our dreams, our hopes, our only chance of keeping the ball club together.

We walked out quietly, while Mr. McLeod was shouting at the policeman and at Lenny.

"Now what?" Dick asked.

"Aw, let's go play ball," Jerry said.

"The heck with all grown-ups," Ned said.

I got on the back of Andy's bike and we rode across town to Sampson Park. There were some little kids playing on the big diamond but we chased them off. The little kids never knew why we were so angry. They didn't know that in our mood we would have chased the Detroit Tigers off.

When I got home for supper, Lenny was gone to Detroit. He'd left a note on the table.

Warm up the stew.
See you in the morning.
We're going to beat those guys BADLY
—Lenny

In the morning Lenny was snoring away. "Come on, Music Man," I said, pounding him in the ribs, "we got a ball game today. Last game of the season. Let's get moving."

Lenny groaned.

"Up and at'm," I said, grinning.

He cocked an eye at me. "Go away."

"C'mon, Coach," I said, "We'll forfeit if you don't

show up."

Though what difference that would make I didn't know. Still this would be our last game as a team and I wanted us to go out in style, beating the tar out of the McLeod Builders and their stinker of a coach.

I brought Lenny his coffee and he sat up.

"You want an egg, too?" I asked.

He regarded me. "You're a regular little cook, aren't you?"

"How do you want it? Sunnyside up?"

"Scrambled."

"Wet or dry?"

He laughed. "Get out of here before I pound you."

I made Lenny two scrambled eggs. I'd eaten already. It was almost nine o'clock. This was about as long as I could wait and still get us to the game on time. We ought to be there at nine thirty.

Lenny came in and began eating his eggs.

"C'mon, man," I said, "move it."

"What time's the game?"

"Ten."

"You got an hour."

"We got the equipment bag. We got to have some infield practice. Even if this is the last game for us, we're gonna go out right."

He looked at me. "All finished with baseball, huh?"

I shrugged. "There's other sports. Football's almost as good a game."

"I never thought I'd hear old Jake Wrather say

something like that. Anyway, if you don't make a living at being a jock, you can always cook. Who do I pitch today?"

"Jerry Jones. He's allowed to go six innings. Tony Parker if Jerry gets wild. C'mon, we got to hustle. That Mr. McLeod won't let us have the diamond anymore than he can get away with."

"I guess you don't like him much."

I looked up at Lenny. "I'm gonna stomp that team today like I never stomped anyone before. Any guy who gets in my way is gonna end up on his back."

Lenny whistled.

"It ain't funny," I said.

"Didn't say it was."

"Good. Here's a cap for you. Today for this last game you're gonna look like a coach."

Lenny laughed; I didn't. I had murder in my heart. I went out to the car to wait for him. In a couple of minutes he came out, wearing the cap, a pair of cut-off football pants, and an old varsity basketball shirt from the University. He looked all right. I liked the way he looked and told him so.

"Well, we go out in style together then, old Jake," he said.

"That's right," I said, and we drove off to Vets Park where the make-up game was to be held.

12.

THE MAKE-UP GAME WAS SET FOR 10 AM. LENNY AND I got to Vets around a quarter to ten, which was much too late. The McLeod Builders had the diamond and Mr. McLeod was hitting the ball around the infield. Our guys were lying in the grass watching.

"Calm down, Jake," Lenny said, before I could say anything. He lifted the equipment bag out of the car trunk with one hand, took out the smaller ball bag and dumped a whole bunch of balls on the ground.

Where we were in the parking lot was about three hundred feet from the diamond.

"Hey, you guys," Lenny shouted, "on your feet and loosen up."

Then he started firing baseballs at our guys. You should have seen them jump. Those balls came like bullets into them. Tony Parker let a shot go through his legs. Danny backhanded a hard one. Jerry ducked under one, but they were moving all right. What an arm Lenny had. The whole McLeod team stopped practice and watched. Even Mr. McLeod stood there gaping.

When the ball bag was empty, Lenny hoisted the heavy equipment bag onto his shoulders and winked at me. "That ought to give them something to think about."

Every eye was on Lenny as he walked across the diamond. We were making an entrance all right. If this didn't psych the Builders out, nothing would.

Mr. McLeod looked over at us. "You want the diamond?" he asked.

Lenny looked at him coldly. "We'll take the diamond when the game starts," he said.

The umps were staking the bases; they kept stealing looks at Lenny, and talking to each other.

Andy and I loosened up along the sidelines. We ignored the McLeod infield practice.

"Who's missing?" I asked.

"Fulton and Bigler."

"Nuts."

You can't start a game with less than eight men. Bigler we could always play without, but John was our catcher. We didn't have another catcher.

"What time's it?"

"Game time almost."

"They couldn't have forgot."

Lenny, the umps, and Mr. McLeod were meeting. I heard Lenny say: "You mean to say any ball into that high grass in right field is an automatic double, even if the guy's rounding second when the ball's got in there?"

"That's right," the ump said.

"I think Bigler had to go to the doctor this morning," Danny said.

"Here they come," Dick shouted. "Both of them." Chugging across the park on bikes as though their lives depended on it, which they did, because if we forfeited the last game the Print-Alls would ever play as a team, I would have strangled them both—came John Fulton and Jeff Bigler.

We were a team.

Lenny called us over.

"C'mon," I called to Bigler and John, "you guys are late."

"We thought it was at West Park."

"You thought," I sneered. "Our last game and you go to the wrong park."

"We're here on time," Jeff said.

"Barely."

"Quiet all of you," Lenny said. "I got to deliver myself of a few deep words."

We gathered around him for the final pep talk. Lenny towered over us. It was like listening to a speech from the Empire State Building. I was used to it, but the other guys weren't.

"Unlike the last game, men, we got all morning to win this one. And we got to win it because it looks like this is going to be the last game for you guys as a team. So let's go out big. Jake, what's the lineup?"

"Kohl, shortstop, Parker second, Wrather third, Black right field, Jones pitching, Fulton catching, Bigler first, Williams center, Franks left."

"Hey," Ned said, "how come you put your home run hitter batting ninth?"

Ned would never let us forget his crazy home run in

the rain-out against Baer Machine.

Everyone laughed. It may have been the last game but we were the same old Print-Alls, and we'd be going out like we came in, having fun, playing hard-nosed, tough, winning ball.

"We're home team," Lenny said. "Same signals as last game. That means no signals at all. Every guy up there swings away; I don't want to see anyone taking fat pitches. You bunt when you want to. Look over their infield. If their third baseman is laying back, drop it in there on him. Base runners steal on their own. Batters, if you see a guy stealing, help him out by taking a cut at the ball. Fuss the catcher. No arguing with the umps. Jake and I will do all the arguing. And lay off the opposing coach, Mr. Bigler. He's a sensitive type. Any questions?"

"Do we swing on 3 and 0?"

"If the pitch is fat, you not only swing, you hit it. But if you pop it up on 3 and 0, I'm gonna beat your butt after the game. Now look, I know what happened the last time you played these guys, but this is a new game, with new umps, and you got yourself a new coach for this last game. For you guys and for me, the season ends right here. So let's pour it on them. Let's show these guys who'd been the league champs if they'd let us play. Git out there!"

We let out a shout, like a football team, and ran onto the field. The McLeod team watched us quietly. I don't know what they were thinking. I didn't care. The stands started filling up with their parents. Usually not too many folks come to watch a Saturday morning make-up game, but there were lots here now and I guess it was because it was a grudge game and there were hard feelings on both teams.

Jerry threw his warm-up pitches as though his life depended on them. Smoking fast balls over the plate. John Fulton winced. That's how hard Jerry was throwing. The McLeod kids watched silently. I figured we had them beaten before the game started.

"Look alive, Jake," Bigler shouted at me and threw the infield ball across the diamond. It cut in front of Jerry. I got down on one knee like an outfielder, blocked it, and whipped it back across the diamond to him. Third basemen could play their position on one knee. I loved third. Everything about it. It was my spot, my home. I tidied it up, scuffed it, it was my busy little corner. Shortstops and second basemen were roamers, they never got the feeling of a bag, but third base was my dwelling. I was going to miss it. After this game, I was finished with kids' baseball. I wasn't going to let any other team draft me. I'd sit out the rest of the season, or play sandlot ball in the parks, and wait for football to start. The rest of the Print-Alls felt that way, too.

"Batter up," the ump called out.

"Let's go get 'em, gang," Dick called out from center-field.

I looked over to the McLeod bench. "You guys better step lightly up there," I growled at them.

They didn't look at me. They were a quiet bench. Even Mr. McLeod looked quiet. They knew what we were going to do to them.

Old Bigler called out to Jerry: "In one ear and out the other, big Jerry."

"Jerry's been wild lately," John Fulton said quietly and sincerely to Tim Johnson, their lead-off hitter.

Jerry went into his big wind-up. I leaned forward. In the dirt or in the glove, I wondered.

It smacked into Fulton's glove like a rifle shot. "Steeerike!" called the ump.

"Way to smoke'm, big Jerry."

"Picking cherries, Jerry."

"Put the next one in his belly button, Jerry."

"Look out, Batter, he's mad at you guys."

Fact was: Jerry was mad, and his anger was concentrating him. He was bearing down on every pitch. His left leg was coming way out and he was following through, the way Lenny had showed him during the last game.

Tim Johnson watched another fast ball come in for a strike. Then Tim started to choke up on his bat.

Jerry's foot came up, the big motion, and then a change up. Tim was way out in front of it for strike three.

We jeered him and threw the ball around. Maybe we weren't very good sportsmen, but this was our last game, thanks to this team, and our hearts were not kindly.

"Everybody in for the big bunter," Bigler called out as Larry Esch stepped in there.

"Everybody in," I echoed and moved up till I was only fifteen feet from the batter.

"What're you doing, Jake?" Lenny called out.

"Gonna stomp a bunt," I said.

Jerry grinned at me, and we were both remembering how he'd thrown the change-up in the last game to let Esch blast one at my head. But there'd be no change-ups now. There'd just be hard smokers. Jerry threw one by Esch, and on the second pitch old Larry dutifully laid on his drag bunt. I picked it up with my bare hand and threw him out by twenty feet.

"How's that for position?" I said to Lenny.

"You're lucky he didn't ram it down your throat."

"Not him. Not any of these guys."

This, I figured, was going to be a dream game with nothing to interrupt it. No rain, no alarm clocks. We were going to be merciless with the McLeod Builders.

Pat McLeod was up next. He was really their best all-around ball player. He had a good eye and he was unafraid. He always got a piece of the ball. Jerry would have to pitch to corners with Pat. The fast ball hummed in there, outside, and Pat sliced it into left field for a single. A lucky hit!

But it had a big effect on the Builders. It woke them up, and they started chattering. Their clean-up hitter was up now—Jimmy Harris, their big first baseman, a muscle boy who if he ever got hold of it would send it a mile. He swung under Jerry's fast one and popped it up. I called for Tony Parker to take it at second and Tony squeezed it for the third out.

We ran in. "Way to go, man," I said to Jerry. "Gonna win this one big," Jerry said.

"Kohl, Parker, Wrather, Black," Lenny read the batting order. "Let's hit and run."

He went to coach at third. Danny dug in, and we called out to him to wait on the curve. Pat McLeod's fast ball couldn't break a pane of glass, but there was that sweet curve. Once in a while he hung it though, and you could hit it anywhere you wanted to.

Pat threw the curve right at Danny who hung in with it. Danny along with Tony had the best bat control on the team. He had a nifty little swing. He could wait till the very last second, when it seemed the ball was behind him, and then whip the bat around in a tiny arc. The ball shot over the shortstop's head and dropped in front of the left fielder for a single. Danny was on and we were off.

"Here we go, gang."

"So long, Pitcher."

"Your socks smell, McLeod."

"Bring him home, Tony. Ducks on the pond."

"Wait on the curve, Tony."

Danny took a big lead off first, dancing a little to rattle Pat McLeod. When Pat came down, Danny took off for second. Swinging to protect him, Tony hit a soft liner off the end of his bat to Jimmy Harris at first. Jimmy stepped on the bag for a double play.

It was tough luck. Danny had the base stolen by a mile. Instead of having a man in scoring position, we had two outs. You would have thought the Builders had won the game. Their bench was alive; their parents were clapping, and their coach, Mr. McLeod, was standing, waving a fist of approval around at his whole team.

That one play should have been a warning about how this game would go. We were a better ball club than they in every department, and we had every reason to beat them, including the big psychological one—this was our last game and it was their fault—but sometimes you try too hard. I don't know. But right then and there I had the funny feeling this game wasn't going to turn out the way it should.

"Batter up," the ump said.

"Give it a ride, Jake."

"You're meat, man."

I stepped in there and looked out at Pat McLeod, a little poised kid who threw like a machine. Without expression.

Wait on the curve, I told myself.

He wound up and threw the curve right at me. I waited and then ducked away.

"Strike," the ump said.

I gave the ump my hard look.

"Caught the inside corner, Jake," the ump said, with a grin in his voice. "You shoulda stuck in there."

He was probably right. I'd stick in there next time. Pat wound up, and the same pitch came at me. I stuck in there, waited for it to break, and then at the last second when I saw it wasn't, I tried to get out. I didn't make it. The ball hit me on the left shoulder.

"Way to stick in there, Jake," Dick Williams, our team

comedian called out.

"Take your base," the ump said.

"He didn't try to avoid that ball, Ump," Mr. McLeod was protesting.

"Aw, shut up," Bigler called out.

The ump turned to Jeff. "Any more talk like that to an adult coach and you're out of the game."

I stood on first. Ned Franks, coaching there, came over. "You hurt?"

"Naw. He couldn't throw the ball through a paper bag."

Jimmy Harris, their first baseman, grinned. "Jake's tough."

I looked at him, and I felt an old mean hate working its way through me.

"Don't mess with me, kid. I'll stomp on you."

For a second, Jimmy Harris looked to see if I was kidding. When he saw I wasn't, he said softly: "Two can play that game, Wrather."

"Well, start playing." I took a big lead off first. Pat McLeod eyed me, whirled and threw to first. I had his throw beat, but Harris was blocking me. He kept me off the bag. I couldn't get through him or around him. I dove and he brought the ball down hard on my head.

"Out," the ump said.

The Builders started cheering.

I jumped up. "He was blocking me, Ump. That's interference."

The ump turned his back on me. I heard Jimmy Harris laughing. I ran after the ump, my fists doubled up.

"Ump—"

A big hand came out of nowhere and turned me around. Lenny looked down at me, his face without expression but his eyes hard and glittering. "What's the matter, Kid?"

I gulped, breathed out, the anger left me.

"It's a judgment call, Jake. Maybe he blocked you, maybe you slid in the wrong spot. Maybe you'll get a chance to block him, and he'll slide in the wrong spot."

I nodded. I got the point. I turned to Harris. "See you later."

Coming in for their bats, the McLeod Builders jeered me.

"What's the matter, Jake?"

"Can't take it?"

"You're so tough, Jake."

Lenny looked at me. I nodded, got my glove, and went out to third base. This wasn't a baseball game anymore; this was war. That's how they wanted it; it was how they were going to get it.

13.

Fact is: you can't play baseball angry. You can play football angry and really knock down a guy who's bigger and tougher than you, but you get angry in baseball and you get tight.

We were tight. It didn't show at first because Jerry was hot and he mowed down the Builders one, two, three with three strike outs.

But in our half of the inning, there was Andy Black, looking mad up there, swinging for the fence and popping it up. And then Jerry swinging for the fence and popping it up. And John Fulton looking like he could spit, going for a bad pitch and striking out.

Anger wasn't helping us at bat. It didn't help us in the field. One of their kids poked an easy grounder at Danny Kohl. Danny's a regular vacuum cleaner at shortstop, but he let this one go through his legs. He was throwing it before it got to him.

"Come on, guys," Lenny called out, "you're playing like a bunch of girl scouts. Talk it up, easy, relax, loosen up."

Jerry wasn't taking any chances with us though. He struck the next three guys out, and we were in to our bats.

"Let's hear some noise on the bench," Lenny said. We

talked it up, but our hearts weren't there. The easy riding of the other pitcher was gone. We really hated Pat McLeod and his team, and it's hard to ride a pitcher you really hate. I mean—you want to kill him—not rattle him.

Bigler was up. "Do your thing," Jeff," I called out.

We were fooling no one. Jeff's thing was bunting and running. Their third baseman came in. So did their first baseman. Their second baseman shaded toward first to cover the bag if Jeff bunted.

McLeod came in with a couple of bad pitches. He was trying to keep the ball high.

Finally he threw his curve and Jeff bunted it. It was a beautiful bunt because it dribbled to the shortstop side of the charging third baseman. He had to stop, reverse himself, and grab the ball. He got it. But Jeff was tearing for first. Boy, he was fast.

We were shrieking. Go, go, go, go.

Jeff tore across the bag simultaneously with the ball arriving in Harris's glove.

"Safe," the ump shouted.

Mr. McLeod protested, but Jeff was safe. Safe on sheer desire and legs.

We started chattering again. This could do it. This might be the break-through. There wasn't a pitcher and catcher in the eleven-year-old league that could prevent Jeff Bigler from stealing every base in sight.

Pat McLeod had a meeting with his catcher and first baseman. Whatever they were cooking up, it wouldn't work.

Bigler didn't take too much of a lead off first. He didn't need the lead. Besides his reflexes were no good. He could get picked off too easily. All he needed was for Pat to throw his pitch to the plate, and he'd be off with flying feet for second.

Pat threw to first. Jeff got back easily. Pat threw to first again. Again Jeff got back.

"Come on, McLeod, quit stalling."

"He's going, Pat. He's going."

Pat stepped on the rubber, looked over at Jeff who was grinning at him, and then he threw to the plate, wide, a pitch-out.

Jeff was flying. Late start and all, he was flying. The catcher wound up and threw to second. Jeff was in in a cloud of dust. Safe. And for good measure the second baseman dropped the ball.

"He'll steal third, Pat."

"He's coming down, Third Baseman."

"Out of the way, Third."

"Look out, Catch. He's coming."

Pat stepped on the rubber. Looked back at Jeff and threw home. Jeff took off for third and he had such a good jump the catcher didn't even make a play on him. The pitch was a ball.

Two pitches, two bases stolen.

Now, however, came the problem. Jeff could steal home; he had stolen home in the past, but he wasn't a good home plate stealer. Stealing home is a matter of timing as well as speed. And Jeff had practically no timing.

But the way Pat McLeod's curve ball was fooling us, and Dick Williams was one of our weak hitters, it paid Lenny to send Jeff in.

Lenny and Jeff were talking. He was showing Jeff how to go down the line with McLeod's wind-up.

Pat McLeod went over to talk to his father and his father must have told him to forget about the base runner on third and go to a full wind-up. He did. Jeff went down the line. The pitch was in for a strike. The catcher whipped the ball to third, but Bigler dove back safely headfirst. A close play. Lenny was mad at Jeff. He called "time" and had a private conference with him, and I knew he was telling Jeff to go. With the speed Jeff had in those legs, he should be across home plate before Pat's slow curve got there.

Two balls and one strike on Dick Williams. And we all knew Jeff was going on the next pitch. We started shouting. The game was only a couple of innings old, but the tension was thick.

"Look out, Catch. He's coming."

"Watch the balk, McLeod."

"Look out, Pitch."

"Watch those spikes, Catch."

"Get the Band-Aids ready, Coach."

McLeod went to his full wind-up and Jeff went down the line and kept coming, streaking for the plate. Pat tried to throw his fast ball over but Bigler really slid. A beautiful slide. He was safe across the plate and had dumped the catcher. The ball was bouncing around the backstop.

We ran over and picked Jeff up and I kissed him.

Jeff was laughing. Lenny clapped him on the back. "You run as good as you talk, First Baseman."

Dick Williams popped up, so did Ned, and Pat fooled Danny with three straight curves, and we were out, but we had one run, and it was a big one because the way Jerry was pitching no one was going to lay a bat on him. 1-0, isn't as satisfying as 12-0, but today it would have to do.

Jerry stayed hot right till the last inning, and so did Pat McLeod. Neither of them allowed a hit till the top of the sixth when Jimmy Harris walked.

"C'mon, big Jerry," I said, "three more men and we got those guys beat. One, two, three, big Jerry."

All eleven-year-old games in the Arborville Recreation League were six innings long. All we had to do was get three outs and we'd have the Builders beaten.

Don't walk anyone else, I prayed.

I guess I had even forgot how badly I had wanted Jimmy Harris to get on base so I could block him the way he'd blocked me, and put a skull tag on him the way he'd put a skull tag on me back in the first inning.

Jerry gulped for air. The tension was taking a lot out of him, and as a fast ball pitcher, he worked hard. A lot harder than Pat McLeod who looked fresh compared with Jerry.

Jerry kicked the dirt, angry with himself for putting Harris on. That was a bad sign. When Jerry was mad at the other team, he pitched well; but when he got mad at himself, then he got wild.

Sure enough, the next pitch was a shovel pitch. John blocked it beautifully, but Jimmy Harris slid into second.

Lenny came out and talked to Jerry, trying to calm him down. "Just three outs, big man, and we win this game. Forget about the guy on second. Your catcher and third baseman can take care of him. Just pour the fast ball into the catcher's glove and they'll flop for you."

Easier said than done, I thought.

Harris on second called out to me: "Hey, Jake, I'm coming down."

"Come on down, baby," I called back. "I got a real reception waiting for you."

Lenny turned to me: "No funny stuff, Jake. Not with a one run lead and three outs away from victory."

"No funny stuff," I said.

Harris took a big lead. Danny cut for the bag, forcing him back. Jerry, fussed, I think by Harris, threw in the dirt again. John blocked it. I heard Harris coming. Good, I thought. I blocked third and waited for the throw from John. It was right on. I grabbed it and slammed the ball down hard where Harris's head should be. It wasn't there.

He'd fooled me. He'd set me up for the same play he'd pulled on me at first base and then hooked-slid around me.

"Safe," the ump called.

"Come on, Jake," Lenny said angrily, "you got to look where your man is."

Harris lay there grinning at me. "Nice try, Jake," he said.

I looked at him a second. I could have piled into him and busted his face up good for him. I could take him. I knew it. But he wanted me to take him. He wanted me out of the game. That was the only way they could beat us. Getting us thrown out of the game.

I forced a smile onto my face. "You'll get yours, fat boy," I said.

"When?"

"Anytime you want it."

"Wait till after I steal home," he said, wiping himself off.

I went over to the mound.

"Listen, let's pick him off third. You throw to me on the next pitch. I'll keep him off the bag."

"Nah," Jerry said.

"Shut up and throw to me," I said angrily.

Jerry shrugged.

On the bench Lenny was watching silently. I knew he was going to let me work this out by myself.

Jerry stepped on the rubber. He came to a set position. Harris took a lead down the line. I broke for third. Jerry whirled and threw to me. We had Harris off base all right. We had him thirty feet off base. We had him stealing home. Too late, I threw home. Wild. Way over John Fulton's head. They had the tying run. They were going wild. Jumping up and down, screaming, congratulating Harris. They should have congratulated me. I had given it to them. I'd been suckered into two dumb plays.

Lenny called "time," and came out to the mound. He beckoned me over.

"You ready to start playing baseball, Jake?"

He turned to Jerry. "Just get it over, big man. Get these three guys out and we'll get that run back. We got the top of the lineup up."

Jerry was fussed though. He was kicking the dirt. He was mad at me. He kept looking at me. I couldn't meet his eyes. I felt lousy. I was giving away the whole season right now.

Lenny tried to calm Jerry down, but when he started pitching again, his whole rhythm was gone. He walked the next batter, and Lenny came out again and brought in Tony. Jerry went to play second.

The McLeod bench was all chatter. They had the momentum now. They had no doubt they were going to beat us. We were tight and they were loose. We were making mistakes, they were not. They had no outs and a man on first, and our star pitcher was out of there.

"Play at second," I called out, when Tony was finished warming up. "Look out for the bunt."

It was the right strategic move, and the kid bunted. It was a good bunt, but I thought I might have a play at second. I picked it up, whirled and threw. Too late. Another bonehead play. Get the sure out. The sure out.

I took a deep breath. Their bench was riding me.

"Hey, Jake. Nice play, Jake. Thanks for the gift, Jake. You're soooo tough, Jake."

They were laughing. Our guys were silent. We could feel the game oozing out of our hands.

"C'mon, gang," I shouted, "let's make some noise."

But you couldn't buy noise from our guys. There was

this strange feeling that a team we should be stomping on was going to beat us and not a thing we could do about it. Even I had the feeling, and I hated it.

Tony threw a curve that hung out there. The batter hit a sizzler down toward me. I had a play at third, but the ball was too hot to handle. I got down in front of it, knocked it down with my chest, jumped for it. Too late for third. I fired it across the diamond to get the one at least.

"Nice play, Jake," Lenny called out.

"You can always use your chest even if you can't use your head," Jimmy Harris said.

Nuts to you, I thought.

"One away," I said.

Men on second and third.

"Let's hold them, guys."

"Infield in," Lenny called out. "We got a play at the plate."

I moved in. In a spot like this I wished old Jerry were pitching, because they got around only too easily on Tony's half-speed pitches.

Tony went to a full wind-up and threw. Outside. The runner scampered back to third. He wouldn't be going. Not with only one out. A fly ball could bring him in.

Tony threw again. A strike around the knees.

We talked it up. Maybe we could get out of this yet. This was one of their outfielders, not a very good hitter.

Tony came down, a nice fat pitch. Oh, no, I thought. The kid stepped into it, but hit under it sending a high fly into short left field. The runner was tagging up. Ned had a pretty good arm. We could get out of this one.

"Home," I shouted at Ned. Ned grabbed at the ball, started to throw, and never caught the ball properly, it dribbled down between his glove and his hand. He was too anxious to throw. The runner scored easily. 2-1, their favor.

Ned threw the ball in to Danny, and I thought he was going to cry.

It was my fault. I shouldn't have shouted at him. I'd rattled my own teammate.

"We'll get it back, Neddy. I swear to you we'll get it back."

The McLeod team was congratulating their runner. Mr. McLeod was shaking hands with everyone as though the game was over.

"We got last licks," Bigler said to them.

"You can have them," they laughed.

You could have heard a pin drop on our side of the field. Not a word from any of us.

Even when the next batter dropped a surprise bunt, and John made a beautiful play on him, throwing him out at first, not a word to John. Two out. Men on second and third. We weren't out of this mess yet.

The next batter was Tim Johnson, their lead-off man. The Builders were yelling for more runs. Tim could hit Tony. Anyone could hit Tony. Tim stepped into an outside pitch and hit a shot down the first base line. To this day I don't know how Bigler knocked it down, but he did, and beat Tim to the base. Three out. And we were lucky. Lucky they'd only got two runs. No, they hadn't got anything. We'd given them two runs. We walked in slowly. Pat McLeod, grinning, went out to the mound.

"OK, guys," Lenny said, "this is it. The whole season in this last licks. Let's get on base."

I went over to Danny. "Danny, you get on and I'll drive you in. I swear I will."

He nodded, but he didn't look cheerful. Pat McLeod looked fresh as a daisy out there. He looked as though he could throw those tantalizing curve balls all day and night.

Danny tried to fool them. He drag bunted the first pitch, but it went foul. After that he took a high curve for a strike, and we knew he was a set-up then. He popped up to the first baseman.

I went up to Tony who was swinging two bats.

"Tony, you get on and I'll drive you in. I swear I will. You got to get on."

Tony nodded, chewing on his gum. He threw one bat away, adjusted his batting helmet and stepped in. He swung with a choked bat. He could follow Pat's curve ball around. He'd hit it. Tony could hit anyone.

"It's a nothing ball," I shouted. "Just stick with it and stomp it."

The pitch came in, lazy and tricky. Tony waited and then his bat came around. We jumped up. The ball flew off it like a shot and then smack—right into Pat McLeod's outstretched glove.

Two out. One out away from defeat in our last game ever as a team, our big revenge game. The Print-Alls were going down.

I looked over at Lenny. He winked at me. "He's easy to hit, big Jake. Just watch it down the slot and meet it. Just meet it."

Yeah, I thought, grimly, just meet it.

Their bench, and their team in the field started riding me.

"Hey, batter, batter."

"Look out, Jake."

"In one ear and out the other, Pat."

They were imitating us. They'd become us; we'd become them. Suckered, psyched out, and beaten.

I stepped out of the box and put some dirt on my palms. They were sweating. Then I stood up and tried to force the tension out of my body. Gonna hit this guy, I thought. Just relax and let the ball come down the slot and meet it where it's pitched and come all the way home. All the way home.

"Up to you, Jake," Jerry called out softly.

"Come on, tough guy," Andy Black said. "You can do it for us, man."

I stepped in, never taking my eyes off Pat McLeod. No quick pitches this game. If he was going to get me out, it would have to be honestly.

"No batter, Patty," the catcher called out. "Jake's no hitter."

The first pitch was a curve that broke too soon and

down. Ball one.

I stepped out again and looked at their outfield. There was a big hole between right and center. If I timed the ball right I could hit it easily between them.

No, I thought, just hit it and forget about trying to place it. I stepped in again. Bat back, elbow up, watch the ball all the way, from the time it leaves Pat McLeod's hand to where it reaches my strike zone and watch it hit my bat. And stomp it good.

The ball left Pat's hand. It was my pitch. I knew it instantly. A good sweet curve already hanging fat in front of the plate, a little to the outside. In my groove. I swung easily, hitting it with the fat of my bat. It was off to right center. I was halfway to first and they were still chasing the ball. The Print-Alls were screaming, so were the McLeod Builders. Parents were shouting. Lenny's voice cut through it all. "All the way, Jake. All the way."

This was it. I was going all the way and if there was gonna be a play at the plate, that catcher was going to have to make that tag ten feet in the air because I was going to stomp him good.

I headed to third. The ball was on its way back to the infield. I looked up at Lenny.

"Hold it, Jake!" he shouted. Hands up. "Whoah …"

The ball wasn't near me, so I made my turn and held up. Their second baseman had it. He pivoted and threw to the plate. A hard low throw … I started moving. It could go through the catcher. It did. He ran to the backstop. I put on steam and headed home, knees high, elbows flying, pounding the earth. Pat McLeod had run in and was covering home. He was standing there with his back to me waiting for the throw from the catcher. I had Pat cold. I had him cold and unprotected. I didn't even have to slide. All I had to do was hit him with my shoulder and he was out of baseball for the year. Stomp him, Wrather. Stomp him!

"Look out, Pat," someone shouted.

In a flash of a second I saw Pat's face, twisted and frantic, the ball was in his hand. He was trying to get out of the way of my hurtling body.

I don't know what happened next. I mean, I know what happened, but I don't know why. In mid-air, I twisted like a diver doing a half-gainer, dropped my shoulder, my whole body to the ground to avoid his body, to slide around him. It was too late to do it. My left foot caught on the plate. I felt a streak of pain shoot up my leg, and then a thud of someone landing on me, then Lenny's voice and that was all I heard.

The rest was blackness.

14.

You're supposed to see stars when you get clobbered. I didn't see stars; I didn't see a thing. Just blackness, and then voices talking, and I knew I was being carried somewhere. I tried to talk, to tell them I was OK. Was I safe at home? Pat McLeod hadn't tagged me. I was the tying run. Where were they taking me? I wanted to go back to third. Unless we'd scored the winning run, too. Wouldn't someone tell me if we'd won or not?

Then a smash of pain in my leg, and I yelled and then darkness again. That was all I felt. Pain and darkness … and we were driving somewhere. Then I was lifted again … and a new voice and then a friendly soothing darkness with nothing more to worry about.

When I woke up, the first face I saw was Lenny's. He was standing there like God Almighty, looking worried at me. When I saw that old worried expression, I grinned.

"What's the matter, Coach?"

He nodded. "You're one tough kid, Jake."

"What happened?"

"You broke your leg. That's what happened."

"I know that, man. I mean, what happened in the game?"

Lenny started to laugh. He sat down and put his hand

on my head. "Jake, I really think you're going to take care of me in my old age."

I didn't know what he was talking about. All I knew was that he hadn't answered my question.

"OK, guys," Lenny said. "You can come in now."

Then they were all there: Jerry, Andy, John Fulton looking worried as usual, Danny and Tony, Dick and Ned, Bigler biting his lip and saying: "Why didn't you hit that kid, Jake? You wouldn't have broke your leg if you'd hit Pat!"

"Shut up, Bigler," I said.

Everyone laughed.

"That means Jake's OK," Dick said.

"Can't hurt old Jake," Jerry said, grinning at me. Lenny looked up. "Out of the way, guys. We got a couple of visitors."

The guys stepped to one side, and there was Pat McLeod and behind him his father. What were they doing here?

Pat stood there, smiling awkwardly. "Hello, Jake," he said.

"You," I growled. "We'll get another crack at you guys next season."

"No," Mr. McLeod said, all red in the face as usual, "not next season. This season. I was all wrong about you, Jake Wrather. That was the gutsiest thing I've ever seen anyone do in my life, what you did coming into home plate. I was wrong about you, about all you boys. Jake, you're out of it for a while with that leg, but your team isn't. The Print-Alls can have that warehouse. Your uncle is going to use it as a music studio so he'll be able to stay in town and coach your team all season. And I'm going to root for you to get better, Jake Wrather, before the end of the season so we can play off today's tie ball game."

I looked at him and at Pat who was nodding and Pat's eyes looked funny and moist. I looked at Lenny and Jerry, Andy, Bigler, John Fulton, Danny, Tony, Ned and Dick . . . they were all grinning at me and their eyes were wet, too.

I tried to take it all in: the tie game, the warehouse, Lenny to coach us, no more Detroit, they can't split us up —as a team, as a family...

"To answer your question, Jake," Lenny said softly, "you scored."

My eyes started getting wet, too. I closed them so nobody could see. I wanted to say we'd all scored, but I couldn't. Not without crying like a baby. And besides I suddenly felt tired, real tired.

I heard another voice then—the doctor's voice—shooing everyone out of the room. In a few seconds the room was empty and silent. It was then that I started to cry. Like a big old baby. I wasn't crying 'cause anything hurt, 'cause nothing did. I wasn't crying 'cause we didn't win, 'cause we did win—we were still a team. I guess I was crying because something had ended on the diamond this morning.

My name is Jake Wrather and I'd always believed you only got what you took for yourself.

Today I hadn't taken, but I'd got. We'd all got. And sometimes that's harder to take and understand than anything else.

I heard the door open. It was Lenny. He came in and sat down next to me. We looked at each other. He took out a big old handkerchief and wiped my eyes. He didn't say a thing. I would have socked him if he had. There wasn't anything left to say. The only thing left now was to get better and rejoin the team.

They'd have to play for a while with only eight guys, but if any team could do it—the Print-Alls could.

I fell asleep with Lenny's big old handkerchief wiping the wet stuff off my face.

About the Author

Alfred Slote has written over thirty books, mostly for young readers. He lives in Ann Arbor, Michigan which has been the setting for his baseball books. He and his wife Hetsy have three children and seven grandchildren. His most recent book, *Finding Buck McHenry*, was made into a Showtime movie.

Other Books For Young Readers by Alfred Slote originally published by HarperCollins:

Baseball Books
Hang Tough, Paul Mather
Tony And Me
Matt Gargan's Boy
Stranger On The Ball Club
The Biggest Victory
My Father, The Coach
The Trading Game
Make Believe Ball Player
Rabbit Ears

Science Fiction
My Robot Buddy
C.O.L.A.R
The Trouble on Janus
Omega Station
My Trip To Alpha 1
Clone Catcher

Other Fiction
A Friend Like That
Moving In

Other Books For Young Readers by Alfred Slote:

Hockey
The Hot Shot
(originally published by
Franklin Watt)

Tennis
Love and Tennis
(originally published by
Macmillan)

Science Fiction
The Devil Rides With Me and
Other Stories
(originally published by
Methuen)

Non-Fiction
The Moon in Fact and Fancy
(originally published by
World)

The Air in Fact and Fancy
(originally published by
World)

Made in the USA
Lexington, KY
17 September 2017